Just Add Mischief

AN
Everly Falls
NOVEL

Just Add Mischief

HEATHER B. MOORE

Copyright © 2023 by Heather B. Moore
Paperback edition
All rights reserved

No part of this book may be reproduced in any form whatsoever without prior written permission of the publisher, except in the case of brief passages embodied in critical reviews and articles. This is a work of fiction. The characters, names, incidents, places, and dialogue are products of the author's imagination and are not to be construed as real.
Interior design by Cora Johnson
Edited by JL Editing Services and Lorie Humpherys
Cover design by Rachael Anderson
Cover image credit: Deposit Photos #116589368/Christina Pauchi
Published by Mirror Press, LLC
ISBN: 978-1-952611-33-9

EVERLY FALLS SERIES:
Just Add Romance
Just Add Mischief

PINE VALLEY SERIES:
Worth the Risk
Where I Belong
Say You Love Me
Waiting for You
Finding Us
Until We Kissed
Let's Begin Again
All For You

PROSPERITY RANCH SERIES:
One Summer Day
Steal My Heart
Not Over You
Seasoned with Love
Take a Chance

HISTORICAL TITLES:
The Paper Daughters of Chinatown
The Slow March of Light
In the Shadow of a Queen
Under the Java Moon
Until Vienna
Love is Come
Esther the Queen
Ruth
The Moses Chronicles
Mary and Martha
Hannah

Just Add Mischief

New neighbor? No, thank you. Peace and quiet? Yes, please.

Fresh from a broken engagement, the last thing Brandy Kane wants is to deal with her standoffish new neighbor, even if his dog is a sweetheart.

Ian Hudson doesn't like people, which includes the busybody family who's apparently moving into the property below his private cabin. A place he thought was abandoned for good. He's secluded himself for a reason, and he isn't about to allow his peace to be disturbed.

But when the rest of his teetering world takes a nosedive, his new neighbor might be the only one to get him through. It will just take adding a little mischief.

One

PEOPLE.

Ian Hudson could hear *people*.

Duke barked, and Ian snapped, "Hush, boy."

Not that he was opposed to people in general, but he'd bought acres of this hillside in order to have peace and quiet. When he wanted to hear other people, he could drive into Everly Falls, grab a meal, get a haircut, buy some groceries. But when he was home and working on his newfound hobby, he didn't want to be disturbed by chatter or the sound of cars passing by or a lawn mower.

A woman's laugh bounced against the walls of his woodworking shed. Well, it was a full-blown workshop, with state-of-the-art machinery. Something he'd invested in a year ago when everything in his life had upended. Ironically, he was fine with the sounds *he* made, whether he was constructing a piece of furniture or repairing something.

Duke pressed his nose against the low window of the workshop, as if he could see through the sawdust film on the glass. He whined, hoping for what would not happen. There was no way Ian was letting the golden retriever out of the workshop, because he'd just bound toward the people and act like he had a set of new best friends.

How close were the people outside? There wasn't another house or cabin for a couple of miles, unless one counted the old Miller place. It was more of a cottage near the main road—which was the only paved road around. The Miller cottage hadn't been available for purchase, since the county owned the property that ran parallel to the rural highway. Ian had inquired.

Maybe they were hikers, and they'd pass by in a couple minutes. He should just return to his work. Instead, he pulled off his safety goggles. "Stay here, Duke, and no barking," he commanded the dog, despite his soulful brown eyes begging to come along.

Ian strode out of the workshop. A quick glance around didn't show the hikers—but he could still hear their voices. Two women, it sounded like. Then a lower rumble followed. A man was with them, too.

Curious, Ian strode along the path that connected to the narrow dirt road that led to his cabin in one direction, then to the main road in the other direction, right past the old Miller place. Perhaps the hikers had already finished their excursion and had come across the quaint cottage. It needed a lot of work to ever be inhabitable, but any passerby could see the charm of the place.

Ian wasn't planning on speaking to the hikers or introducing himself. He just wanted to make sure they weren't going to snoop around. Or heaven forbid, trespass on his own property. Through the trees, he spotted a wide swath of color that had to be a car. Red, to be exact. And another color. White. Belonging to a truck.

The voices were louder now, cheerful, and there was a lot of walking back and forth.

Ian's gut twisted. *No* . . . The next few steps brought three people into clearer view—two women and a man. And they were . . . moving stuff into the cottage.

They couldn't be squatters. Their vehicles and clothing and furniture negated that idea. Then who were these people, and what gave them the right to move into an abandoned cottage? Surely, nothing in that place worked—was the water and sewer even hooked up? Not to mention the electricity.

Ian set his hands on his hips, debating whether to call the county offices, or to confront the trio himself. It was Saturday, so it might be hard to get the county office to answer the phone—unless he called the emergency number. Which was probably reserved for forest fires. And this wasn't exactly an emergency . . .

With a heavy sigh, Ian cut through the trees, taking the shortcut path to the cottage. He knew his approach wouldn't be silent—there were too many fallen autumn leaves that crunched under his boots. When he emerged, he found three people staring at him.

"Oh, you scared me," one of the women said. Her sandy-blonde hair was tied up in a peach-colored scarf, and her shirt was a kaleidoscope of colors he probably couldn't name.

The other woman stood on the porch, shaded by the roof. She held a box on her hip and didn't seem all that startled. Her gaze was curious, and she took her time scanning him from head to foot.

He probably had sawdust in his hair, and his work jeans were not much cleaner. He was pretty sure the T-shirt beneath his flannel shirt had wood stain on it—no amount of laundry detergent could ever get it out. Not that he cared about the state of his clothing and hair, but he knew plenty of people in Everly Falls were quick to judge—small town and all.

Maybe he should have moved to a big city—he'd be more anonymous—because by the looks of it, his carefully arranged tranquility and peace had come to an end.

The man stepped forward. Dark hair, dark eyes, around six two, which set him a couple of inches shorter than Ian. "You the neighbor up the road?" the man asked.

His expression was friendly, open, and that annoyed Ian. He wasn't interested in chitchat or making friends.

"Neighbor?" Ian rasped. "To whom?"

The man swept a hand toward the woman on the porch. She was still standing in the shade of the roof, but he could see that she was blonde, pretty in a high-maintenance way, and petite enough that she'd probably blow away in the next storm coming through the hills.

"Brandy's moving in today," the man continued. "We heard there was a resident up here."

"You mean a recluse," the woman with the peach scarf said with a laugh. She turned her smiling hazel eyes on Ian. "You look normal enough, though."

He must not be doing his best glower, so he folded his arms. "And you all are . . . ?"

"I'm Austin Hayes, and this is my fiancé, Everly Kane."

Ian's frown deepened. "Everly, as in Everly Falls?"

The peach-scarf woman waved away his question. "Yeah, sure. It's old news. This is my sister, Brandy. Seems like you've got a new neighbor."

Brandy still hadn't spoken, but her eyes remained locked on him.

"You're Ian Hudson, right? The retired financier?" Everly continued. "Don't see you in town much."

"Don't go to town much," he deadpanned, keeping his arms folded. "I thought this was county property. Are you, uh, employed by the county? Are they renting to you or something?"

Please say yes, and please say that no one is actually moving into the cottage, and I won't have any neighbors.

"Nope," Everly said. "My sister is moving in. She went through a recent, uh, life event and other things, and my mom begged her to stay in Everly Falls, and this was a compromise."

Ian wasn't sure of all that Everly had said, but she hadn't answered his question.

"You're *not* renting? The county wouldn't sell to me—so why would they sell to you?" Maybe Ian was being rude, but he needed to know.

"Here's the thing," Everly said as Austin came to stand by her. The pair linked hands. "My great-grandad built this place, and when the county bought his property from him, the deed stated that his descendants could still live here until the county develops the land." She spread her arms. "Nothing's developed, so here we are."

Ian knew he was frowning, but this was all news to him. How did he not know about the deed? "I thought you said your last name was Kane."

"Miller is our mother's side," Everly clarified.

Ian rubbed the back of his neck. So. The waif of a woman standing on the porch, apparently mute, was moving into this dilapidated cottage. Maybe she was a quiet person? Unlike her chatty sister?

"I'm *so* glad you'll have such a close neighbor, Brandy," Everly said. "We could come up for barbecues and other neighborly activities." She grinned at Ian, then Austin. "What do you think, guys?"

"Sounds good to me," Austin said, his mouth quirked.

Both Brandy and Ian remained mute.

"I could use a hand if you've got a little time," Austin added, motioning toward the bed of the truck. Furniture pieces had been strapped in, and they would definitely be awkward for a person to carry single-handedly.

And that was how Ian ended up not only meeting his new neighbor, but also helping her move in.

Two

"WHERE DO YOU WANT THIS?" a low voice asked.

Brandy turned from where she'd just set down a box on the kitchen counter, which had seen better days.

Ian Hudson filled the entire doorway of the cottage, carrying a box marked "Kitchen."

Brandy tapped the counter. "Here is fine." She didn't have a lot of possessions, and they'd been more than halfway done when Ian had showed up. She'd cringed when Austin had asked for his help because the man's scowl seemed to be a permanent feature on his face.

When he'd strode out of the woods, she thought she'd gone back a few hundred years in time, and Paul Bunyan had just appeared. She'd heard about Ian Hudson, of course. Moved to Everly Falls last year sometime. Brandy had been planning her wedding to Brock Hayes and hadn't paid much attention to the town gossip. Now, she wished she could at least remember something.

She wondered how a financier—a geek, in other words—had the build of a pro-athlete. The breadth of his shoulders made him look like he could uproot one of the pine trees outside her cottage with his bare hands.

Brandy tried not to stare as Ian strode toward her now, his boots clomping on the bare hardwood floor, which needed a good sanding and probably new stain. Despite olive skin, his dark hair and dark glower, his eyes were a surprising light green. Right now, they were icy, and he seemed to have no problem returning her stare.

"Thanks," she said as the box thumped on the counter. "I think we're good from here. Appreciate your help, though."

Ian and Austin had carried in all the furniture already, and now Austin and Everly were outside, cutting back the overgrown bushes in front of the house. Brandy had told them it could all wait until next weekend, but Everly hadn't listened to her.

"You staying long?" Ian asked.

This close up, Brandy had to lift her chin to meet his gaze. How tall was he? At five seven, Brandy wasn't a shrimp, but this guy was really tall. And did she mention he was built? Like he didn't spend any of his time on the couch. No TV series bingeing for this man.

Not like Brock, her ex, who spent hours in the gym to bulk up. No, this man had a more natural build.

"What do you mean by *long*?" Brandy asked. No matter the size of this mountain man, she wasn't going to let his hard tone and direct questions bother her. She had no problem throwing questions back into his face. Who did he think he was anyway? She was legitimately here, and he could stay on his *own* property, and out of her way.

Brandy wasn't exactly familiar with this section of the hills. The waterfall hikes were several miles down the road, and she didn't know if she'd been up this way much since she was a kid, and they'd drive by "Grandpa's cottage" every so often.

Ian rested one of his large hands on the edge of the counter. "You don't look like the nature type. Maybe living in the woods is fun for a short vacation, but you're moving a lot of stuff into this cottage. Tells me you're staying longer than a week or two."

Brandy folded her arms. "*Nature type?* What do you mean by that?" Again, she was asking a question instead of answering *his* questions. She didn't know why she wanted to irk the man, except he'd irked her. Blasting out of those trees like he owned the place, suspicion in those clear green eyes of his. Not to mention his perpetual scowl and accusatory words.

"I mean . . ." His voice trailed off as he scanned her person, from the flip-flops she wore to her yellow capris and white-and-yellow blouse, to the strand of pearls at her neck. His gaze lingered, then lifted again to her face.

She felt a blush coming on, not because this man's perusal of her person was flattering, but because she was angry that he was judging her. He sounded like her mom. *Why would you want to live so far from civilization? You don't even know how to change a flat tire. What if the internet goes out? What if you get sick and can't drive into town to see the doctor?*

It wasn't that Brandy was helpless. She was a grown woman with a college accounting degree. She freelanced as a CPA, and she also worked for a nonprofit that funded wells in Africa. So she didn't need to be in an established office. Yes, she relied heavily on the internet, but she was going to get that figured out with the hot-spot subscription she'd added through her cell phone carrier. She'd been to *Africa* on humanitarian trips—places way more rural and primitive than Grandpa Miller's cottage.

Nature was just that—nature. Trees, leaves, dirt, and rocks.

"You just look more . . ." Ian paused. "Used to the city life."

Brandy was pretty sure he was going to say something else. What exactly, she didn't know, but she could see the contempt, or was it suspicion, in his eyes.

"I love the hills," she said. "I love trees. I love fresh air. And I'm looking forward to a lot of quiet, Mr. Hudson. So despite what my sister Everly said, I'm not interested in being neighborly. Sorry if that hurts your big, fat ego, but count me out of any neighborhood barbecues."

Ian's hard gaze shifted. His dark glower was gone, and the ice faded from his eyes. Then his mouth turned up at the corners, making his entire expression change. Brandy could admit that her brutish neighbor was handsome in a hunk-of-a-man way, but Ian Hudson smiling made something deep inside her chest heat up.

"Perfect, Ms. Kane." Ian stepped away from the counter. "You won't have to worry about being neighborly, because the entire reason I live on acres of land by myself is because I want quiet, too."

Triumph zinged through Brandy. "Well, then, I guess we agree. Again, thanks for your help, and I'd say, 'See you around,' but I hope that doesn't happen."

Ian's smile spread.

That smile could weaken a woman's knees. Not Brandy's, of course. Handsome men were on Brandy's *completely ignore* list. Her heart had been shattered in so many pieces that she didn't even know where those pieces had ended up.

Ian's low voice rumbled in the silence between them. "Have a good, uh, week, Ms. Kane."

"You, too, Mr. Hudson."

She watched him turn and walk out of the cottage, which had seemed to shrink with him inside of it. Her breath escaped as the screen door banged behind him and his boots pounded across the porch. She heard a short conversation between the men, then Everly's voice piped up. Whatever they said, Ian Hudson disappeared moments later—back into the woods where he'd come from.

Finally.

Now, Brandy had to convince her sister and almost brother-in-law that she was fine. Bush cutting and porch sweeping could be done another day. Right now, she wanted to arrange her kitchen, make some orange tea, and watch the sun set on her first evening of her new life.

Heading out onto the porch, Brandy paused to see Everly and Austin *not* working, but standing together in an embrace, as if they'd just been kissing.

"Oh sorry, did I interrupt?" Brandy teased.

Everly looked over, her face flushed, but she made no effort to release Austin. "Not interrupting. Sorry, we'll get back to work and—"

"That's the thing," Brandy jumped in. "I think we've done enough hard labor for the day. I want to slow things down for the rest of the day. Tomorrow will come soon enough."

Everly laughed. "You mean Mom will show up?"

"Yep," Brandy said. "I need a quiet night before the storm hits."

Austin chuckled, then he released Everly. They were a striking couple—Austin with his dark hair and warm brown eyes, and Everly's honey-blonde hair and dancing hazel eyes.

Her exuberant personality was a nice contrast to Austin's more serious nature.

Austin turned toward Brandy. "We've got a couple of hours to spare. My daughter is perfectly fine at her friend's house. Give us the hardest jobs."

Brandy held up her hand. "No, you're off the hook. You've done so much already. Really. Thank you so much."

"I get it," Everly said simply. She joined Brandy on the porch and hugged her. "You want some of that peace and quiet you've been craving since your return."

Brandy hugged her sister back. Since the big breakup with Brock and the cancelation of her wedding one week before the big day, she'd taken a work hiatus and spent a couple of weeks at the beach in a town several hours away. When she'd finished nursing her deepest wounds, she let her mom and sister talk her into coming back to Everly Falls.

She'd moved back into her mom's house because that's where she'd been living while engaged to Brock. But the memories around town were too painful. The café where they'd eaten together, the bakery that had been making her wedding cake, the park where they'd taken long walks in the evening . . . And Brock himself still lived in Everly Falls.

She'd blocked his number, of course, but when she saw him in line at Marshall's Coffee early one morning, she knew she couldn't live in town anymore. Thus, the solution of relocating to Grandpa Miller's cottage—which Mom objected to. If anyone would understand, Everly would, since she'd dated Brock first.

Yeah . . . it was a mess.

Brandy was a mess. And she was tired of it. She was going to find her way through it all, though. All she needed was time and quiet and peace, and no nosy neighbors or people staring at her or asking her friendly but intrusive questions.

She didn't need the small town of Everly Falls to watch her faltering her way back to normal. Or *new* normal, she guessed.

"Thanks, sis," Brandy said, releasing Everly. "Seriously, I don't know what I'd do without you."

"Call me with anything you need." Everly drew her cell phone out of her pocket. "I have service, do you?"

Brandy checked her phone. "Yep. It's all good. And I'll be setting up my hot spot tonight, so things will be running smoothly."

"Still." Everly's brow dipped. "If things don't work out here, I can talk to Darla about my old apartment. She's just using it for storage."

"I'll let you know." They'd been over this, though. The makeshift apartment over the craft store where Everly worked wasn't a better solution since it would put her right in the center of town. "Thanks again. Drive safe, and give Jessica a hug for me."

Jessica, Austin's seven-year-old daughter, had wrapped the entire Kane family around her finger. How would it be to be a kid again, with your whole life ahead of you, unaware of two-timing men and broken hearts?

Three

As Duke paced the cabin, Ian knew it wasn't because he was hungry. He had already fed the dog. Although he was now cooking what should be lasagna but looked like a mash-up no-name meal, the dog was trained not to beg for food.

Duke was pacing because he knew they had a neighbor.

"You're not meeting her," Ian grumbled. "Or at least not today. If you do meet her, then it will be by chance. No running over to the cottage and introducing yourself."

Okay, so living as a recluse for the past year might have turned Ian into a person who talked more to his dog than to anyone else. Sure, he dealt with a flurry of emails each morning, but that was the only time he allowed himself to dip back into the real world. Two years ago, just after he and Pete Callahan—his best friend and partner in a data storage company—took their company public, Ian discovered that his lovely wife and his best friend had been having an affair. For months.

Ella hadn't wanted to reconcile, even if Ian could have brought himself to forgive her. She was still with Pete. Not married yet, but that would probably come. Ella had filed for divorce, and Ian had liquidated his majority stock, then stepped down from the company he thought would be his breadbasket until retirement. No longer.

So here he was. Hours away from the people his life used to revolve around. He could live a decent existence for decades if he decided not to work, but not working wasn't in his bones. He'd gone back to his roots and now built custom furniture. Something he swore he'd never do. He couldn't count the number of times his father had begged him to go into business with him—to make Hudson's Furniture into Hudson and Son's Furniture—but Ian hadn't been interested in working in a small town for his dad's furniture shop. No, he wanted to create and build something bigger than a small-town small business.

Irony at its best.

If his dad were still alive, Ian would have had a lot of apologizing to do.

Duke whined as he paused and rested his nose on the windowsill of the kitchen, which overlooked the grassy area before the road. It would be far-fetched to call it a yard or a lawn. But the open space gave Ian a full view of the road leading to the highway, although he couldn't see the cottage from his place. He'd have to walk a couple hundred yards before he could do that.

Not that he was considering dropping in on his neighbor. He was just curious, that was all. Brandy Kane seemed to have a close-knit family, so why did she want to live all the way up here and not in town? Ian had been honest when he told her she didn't seem like the nature-loving type. Her hair was too . . . smooth and shiny. Her makeup a bit too perfect for the wide outdoors. Her clothing too bright and clean. Her fingernail polish and toenail polishes matched. He could easily see her in his former world, where the women were glossy and preening.

Ella had been one of those women.

Ian released a sigh and crossed to Duke. "How about after I eat, we go on a hike? Get the energy out?" His new profession provided plenty of labor for himself, but he knew that Duke appreciated an adventure.

After eating, Ian headed out with Duke, and sure enough, the dog headed straight for the cottage.

"Duke, this way!" he called in a sharp tone.

The dog obeyed, but didn't look happy about it. A few minutes into their hike, Duke's mood lightened, and he went about his business, running ahead and smelling everything in sight. Ian's body heated up, and he took off his flannel shirt and slung it over his shoulder.

He loved the crisp air, the soft breeze, and the only sounds being that of nature and his dog discovering new things. Out here, he could almost forget the pain of the past. His fractured relationship with his father and his completely broken relationship with Ella and Pete. If he thought back, which he tried to avoid, he didn't know what he would have done differently. At least with Ella.

All right. There was a lot he could have done differently—but whatever he'd done, it still hadn't been enough. That was the thing with Ella—there was always *more* that she wanted. More vacations, more decorating, more outings with her girlfriends . . . Ian had gone along with it, because it was what he'd wanted, too. At least in the beginning.

They'd been married five years when Ian first brought up kids. Ironic again. Wasn't the woman usually the one with the biological clock ticking? Ella had laughed and laughed. They'd settled for a dog—which she had ignored.

Duke barked at something, and a lizard scuttled across the path, disappearing into the trees beyond. "Stay on the path," Ian commanded.

The dog's shoulders sagged, but in another few seconds, he was back to sniffing everything with absolute joy. Ian chuckled.

The sun continued to sink, and the sky shifted from its hazy blue to deep gold and burnt orange. Warmth from the early fall afternoon quickly faded, replaced by a cooler temperature. Ian would have to start wearing a jacket in the coming weeks. As it was, he pulled his flannel shirt back on.

Up ahead, Duke reached the boulder that overlooked the next valley over. This was their stopping place, and the dog remembered. Duke leapt onto the rock.

"Good boy." Ian joined him on the boulder.

They sat together for several moments, watching the twilight darken the land. Below was the town of Everly Falls, spread out like a postcard. Ian could probably identify most things just by sight, even though he'd inspected very little of the town itself.

There was a time in his life when he couldn't get away from his hometown fast enough. Everything about it was too quiet, too slow, too backward. His dad never did install Wi-Fi at his home before he died. He was all about the simple life, and it drove Ian nuts.

Suddenly, Duke went on alert. Then he scrambled off the boulder and barked.

"What is it, boy?" Ian looked toward the path, but didn't see anything. He wasn't too worried about wild animals around here—but there could always be a first time. Rising from the boulder, he said, "Don't move, Duke."

The dog was practically trembling, making every effort to obey, but Ian could see it was torture.

Then he heard it. The sound of someone approaching. Human or animal?

His question was answered in the next second when a hiker appeared down the path. It took only a half second for Ian to realize it was Brandy Kane. His not-neighbor.

"Duke, stay," he added for good measure.

Brandy's head snapped up. "Oh, hi." Her hand moved to her chest. "I didn't know there were people up here—or, uh, person." Her gaze skated to the dog. "Hey there." She spoke in a higher-pitched voice, one that most people reserved for their pets.

Duke whined as his tail thumped a hole in the dirt.

"Who's this?" Brandy continued, her gaze still on the dog.

"His name is Duke, and he's been dying to meet you." Now *that* didn't come out like Ian expected.

"Hi, Duke. You're such a beautiful boy." Brandy crouched before the dog and held out her hand. "Can I pet him?"

"Yeah."

So Brandy did just that, and Duke flopped down and turned over on his back. She scratched his belly. "You're a good boy, aren't you?"

Apparently Brandy was a dog person, and Ian didn't know why that pleased him. Ella had barely tolerated the dog. Still, watching Brandy interact with his dog shouldn't be anything interesting. A lot of people were dog lovers. Thousands, or probably millions.

Yet Ian couldn't avert his gaze from Brandy scratching Duke, and Duke acting like he'd never been pet in his life before this very moment. Ian's gaze strayed to what she was wearing. Definitely not hiking clothing. It looked more like... yoga wear? Not something that matched up with trudging through dirt, rocks, twigs, and leaves.

Her white tank shirt was baggy enough to show the peach-colored sports bra beneath, and her leggings were, well, peach, too. That type of outfit belonged in a gym, maybe? She had to be cold, too. Was she cold?

The breeze kicked up just then, as if Mother Nature had heard his thoughts, and goose bumps raced across his neck.

"How old is Duke?" Brandy asked.

"Four next month." Ian crouched on the other side of the dog and scratched his head. From this position, he could look Brandy in the eyes. They were a fierce blue, even in the twilight. "You're going to spoil him."

She laughed. "You can't spoil a dog, Mr. Hudson."

Ian didn't know how to respond because her laugh had somehow warmed his skin. "Do you have a dog? Don't tell me—it's one of those miniature yapping things."

He hadn't seen or heard a dog at the cottage, but maybe it was on its way?

Brandy's brow arched, and she pushed to her feet. He rose, too, more slowly, though. Duke didn't like their change in focus and pressed against Brandy's legs. She stroked his head as she eyed Ian. "Miniature *yapping* things?"

"Yeah, you know, a shih tzu who barks at everything that moves."

She folded her arms. "Are you profiling me, Mr. Hudson? First you say that I'm not the nature type, and now you're pairing me with a small fluffy dog."

Ian didn't know why he wanted to smile, but he did. It took some effort to keep a laugh out of his voice. "I guess I have profiled you. Can you blame me?"

At this, her blue eyes narrowed. "Continue."

Ian hesitated, then waved a hand. "You're all... you

know. Gussied up. I mean, you're wearing white tennis shoes while hiking a dirt path." He shrugged out of his flannel shirt. "Here, you look cold."

She looked down at herself, then raised her gaze to meet his again. "Keep your shirt. I'm wearing workout clothes, and these shoes are old. Also, I haven't washed my hair for three days."

"Okay..."

The edge of her mouth lifted, and a dimple appeared. He wasn't sure if she was going to smile or chew him out some more. He probably deserved the chewing out.

"You're really caught up in appearances, aren't you?" Brandy's arms fell to her sides now. Duke nudged her fingers, and she played with his floppy ear. "It's kind of like you're worried about everything and everyone else around you. That must take a lot of head space."

He stared at her, trying to comprehend if she'd just insulted him or merely psychoanalyzed him. Was she a therapist or something? Or just one of those people who checked her horoscope on her phone before she got up in the morning? *Please, no.*

"Have a nice night, Duke," Brandy said, bending to kiss the top of the dog's head. "Tell your owner he doesn't deserve a sweet, friendly dog like you." Then she turned and began to walk down the path.

Ian stared after her for a few heartbeats. Had she just *kissed* his dog? "Wait, where are you going?"

"Home."

"Home, home? Or the cottage?" Now, why did he say that?

She glanced behind her, a smirk on her face. "The cottage is my home now, *neighbor*."

He opened his mouth, then shut it. "It's almost dark."

She didn't answer, but she was getting farther away.

He started walking, Duke at his side, wagging his tail. "You shouldn't be walking around the hills by yourself in the dark."

Brandy turned at that. "You do." Her voice carried easily in the quiet.

"Yeah, but . . . I know my way and . . ."

"Let me guess. You're a man?"

There was that laugh again. Light, musical. He exhaled. "There could be wild animals."

"Squirrels and foxes? Maybe a rabid racoon?" She laughed more, then continued down the hill, going faster now.

"Stay by me, Duke," Ian grumbled. He could feel the dog's desire to join Brandy.

Was she . . . jogging? Ian stifled a groan and began to jog, too. He'd keep his distance, but he'd make sure she got back to her cottage—unmolested by wild squirrels or sharp-nosed foxes.

Four

BRANDY KNEW IAN HUDSON WAS following her. Yeah, there was only one path leading to his cabin and eventually to the cottage. And yeah, she'd slowed when she'd walked past his cabin earlier. It was obviously a new construction—a year old? Was that what Everly had said?

Brandy had made it a point not to ask her sister questions about Ian. There was already too much of her mom and sister prying with questions like, "How are you doing?" and "Are you ready to date yet?"

She didn't need another man to get over the one who'd torn her heart out and stomped it to little bits. No, she just needed to focus on *herself*. Brandy Kane. The girl who'd sailed through life with dozens of friends, good grades that came easy, and meeting the love of her life soon after she'd started her first career job.

Well, the man she *thought* was the love of her life.

In the beginning, the only wrinkle in the relationship was that he'd dated Everly before he met Brandy. But Brock had sworn he'd never considered Everly as serious-girlfriend material. Everything had been casual. That had all changed when Everly started dating Austin, and Brock apparently had all sorts of feelings come up. Feelings he'd always denied to Brandy.

After she'd called off the wedding, she decided she had to change everything. Well, not her job, but everything else. Once home again, she began looking for other places to live. Inside Everly Falls, but mostly outside of it. Her mother had begged her to stay, so Brandy found a compromise, and here she was. Living in the quiet hills above her hometown, taking a break from her formerly whirlwind social life.

She had no desire to face Brock, a man who was truly a master manipulator. Digging more, she'd found out that he had another Instagram account with a fake name. Who knew what connections he had on there? He was always sugary sweet toward her. They'd never argued, but somehow Brock had changed her mind if she was hesitant or disagreed with him. If he ever praised her, he expected more praise in return. Somehow, he'd used their mutual attraction to suck her into *his* life, his way of thinking, until she'd trusted him implicitly and become his little robot.

She's blocked his number and unfollowed him across all social media. Yeah, she knew that someday, at some point, she'd come face to face with him again. But she wasn't going to put herself in that position on purpose. No . . . she'd be just fine in Grandpa's old cottage by herself.

Ian's footsteps pounded behind her, and she let a smile escape. He was jogging, too—that was the only way he could keep up with her. For being such a grumpy non-neighbor, he was sure invested in overseeing her return to her cottage in the dark. And it was pretty dark, but that was just because there were no streetlights out here. Just moonlight.

Brandy nearly stumbled on a bigger rock on the path, but she stayed upright and continued running. Hopefully,

Ian hadn't noticed. Although if he had, he probably would have shouted at her to slow down. He was kind of bossy that way. Very opinionated, too. Brandy hadn't really known what to make of him the first time he'd appeared that morning—all suspicious, with his curt questions.

But tonight—she'd figured out that teasing him only raised his ire. And it was fun. He was so serious and so intense, but at the same time, worried over small things in a way that showed he possessed a human heart after all.

His cabin came into view, and she noticed he'd thought to turn on the outside lights before he left. Brandy wondered if the cottage porch light was working—she hadn't thought to check before starting on her run. She continued jogging past the cabin and stayed on the road that would take her to the cottage. She knew about the shortcut path now, but the trees would block most of the moonlight, and she'd probably fall for real.

Ian's footsteps continued pounding behind her, and his breathing sounded heavy. Was he out of shape, or was he just a loud breather, or maybe not a runner? All these things she wondered, but didn't stop to ask him. Besides, he didn't look out of shape. Nope. When he'd taken off that flannel shirt of his, she'd seen the way his fitted T-shirt defined his arms and lean torso.

Brandy neared her cottage, and Ian was still behind her. Would he come all the way to her porch? *Please, no,* she thought, but another voice said, *please, yes.* She quieted that voice quickly.

Finally, she slowed as she turned onto the path leading to her wooden porch. Ian had stopped running, too. She continued toward her porch without looking back, even though she was tempted to do so. But she couldn't stop herself from saying, "Good night, Duke," before she headed inside.

Closing the door, she leaned against it and laughed to herself. Ian Hudson probably thought she was rude and ungrateful, but she wasn't going to appease him when she hadn't asked for him to follow her. Besides, there'd been no wild animals on the trail.

Flipping on the light switch next to the door, she glanced about the small living room. Boxes were still packed, but all the furniture was in place, thanks to Austin and Ian. Not that she had a lot. A small couch, a side table, and beyond that, a kitchen table with two chairs. She'd brought a three-drawer dresser and a mattress for the bed frame. Yep, she was keeping her new life simple.

Crossing the room, she picked up her phone where she'd left it charging on the end table. Three missed calls and twenty-five texts—most of them from a group chat of her high school friends. They'd all formed a group chat when she'd returned from college, so her three best friends from high school knew her woes with Brock.

Brandy settled on the couch and opened the strand.

Lori: *When are we doing the housewarming party? I've already ordered the cupcakes.*

Julie: *I can get away tomorrow night when Dave gets off work to watch the baby.*

Steph: *Anytime works for me! I'll figure it out.*

Lori: *Okay, so seven p.m.? Should we carpool?*

Julie: *Yeah, I'll pick everyone up.*

Steph: *I'll be ready!*

All of this planning without Brandy's input—but her friends knew her well. She texted back: *Sounds fun. I'll provide the cottage and the nature sounds.*

Steph replied with a smiling emoji.

Next, Brandy opened Everly's text. *Mom will probably*

call you because Brock stopped by the house. Mom didn't tell him where you're living now, but I think he knows something is up.

Brandy wrote back: *OK, thanks for the heads-up.*

She sent the text, then stared at the darkened window of the cottage. She wasn't worried or scared about living out here so isolated. Brock wasn't anyone to be afraid of—in that way. She just wasn't ready to see him yet. She needed more time. And the fact that he went to her mom's was a pretty serious clue that he'd caught wind of her coming back from her little hiatus. Or maybe it was all a coincidence?

She checked her emails next to see if there was anything urgent. One email was from a client who needed quarterly taxes filed this week. Even though it was after hours, she replied: *I should be able to get everything filed tomorrow. Internet seems to be working fine.*

Only after that did she listen to the three voicemails. All from her mom.

Brandy hit "Call" on Mom's number.

"Brandy! I've been trying to call you. Did your phone die again? You know you can't let that happen, especially since you're by yourself in that terrible cottage. Brock stopped by the house today, but you'd better believe I didn't give out any information on you. I was as polite as possible, but I really wanted to throw something in his face. Too bad I wasn't holding a cup of hot coffee. That man . . . he needs to leave the Kane women alone once and for all. I'm of a mind to speak to Officer Carlton about it, but Everly said that's overkill. She's going to have Austin talk to him tomorrow, so I guess we'll just have to be satisfied with that."

"Hi, Mom," Brandy said. "I'm fine, by the way. Just went for a run."

"Why didn't you take your phone with you? Running

alone in the dark isn't a good idea, you know—"

"I wasn't alone," Brandy said, then groaned to herself. Here came the questions . . .

"Who was with you?"

"Ian Hudson—I'm sure you know more about him than I do."

Her mom fell silent, and Brandy could almost imagine her list of questions growing. "Is he the man Everly said lives in that new cabin?"

"Yep, that's him."

"How old is he, and why does he live like a hermit?"

When her mom took her next breath, Brandy said, "I don't know, Mom. I'll ask him next time I see him. I was out jogging, and he was on the same path, so we headed back home at the same time."

Again, her mom was silent, but Brandy knew it wouldn't last long.

"I want to meet him."

Brandy did laugh then. "All right . . . But I don't think he really wants company. He's sort of a recluse, and he's not into neighborly things."

"What does that mean?"

"Never mind," Brandy said. "Look, I'm beat. Got to get up and work tomorrow, then my friends are heading here for the evening."

"Well, that's good. Everly said she'd bring me up tomorrow to help you unpack."

"I'm mostly done," Brandy said just to stave off her mom. "I didn't have that much to move. How about wait until the weekend to visit? Then I'll be more settled in, and I can show you around."

"Show me around the *woods*?"

Brandy smirked. "I'm sure once you see the place, you'll

be happy for me."

Her mom's voice went soft. "I *am* happy for you, Brandy. It's just that this is a really big change."

"Not exactly by choice, Mom," she said. The word *Brock* hung between them. "I'm doing the best I can right now, and people will just have to be happy that this is my new best."

"Of course, dear. You're an amazing woman, and you have a lot to be proud of." Her mom paused. "Now, the fall festival is coming up, and I hope you can help with Gentry's booth. She depends on you girls. You and Everly can trade off shifts."

Brandy didn't mean to hesitate, but a public event like that could very well include Brock. Would he come? There was a very good chance, and she didn't really want a public meeting with him. Or a private one, for that matter. Her mother was on the committee for the festival, so she had no problem volunteering her daughters to help, which normally Brandy didn't mind.

"I should be able to come," she hedged.

Mom sighed. "If Brock comes, just don't talk to him. Everly can keep a lookout."

"We'll see." Brandy didn't think it was fair to anyone in her family to be on the lookout for her ex. But she didn't want to get into a big debate right now.

"Keep your phone with you so your poor mother doesn't have another heart attack."

"I'll try to remember that," Brandy promised. "Or I'll let you know when I'm going unplugged." She knew her mom would soon stop obsessing over the fact that she had moved to the middle of nowhere. At least she hoped.

After hanging up with her mom, Brandy walked out onto the porch. The moon was nearly full, and the stars spread across the sky like a horde of glittering fireflies. The breeze had cooled everything off, and she folded her arms against the cold. Through the trees, she could see the location of Ian's cabin because of his porch light.

Knowing that she wasn't entirely alone made her feel . . . secure, maybe? At least if there was an emergency, she could ask for help. She had no doubt that Ian Hudson would help in an emergency. He just didn't want any regular neighbor stuff, and she didn't either, so it was all fine.

She moved her gaze back to the sky. She'd been right. It was quiet up here. So very quiet that it felt a bit odd. Maybe she should put on some music? Would Ian hear it? She couldn't hear anything coming from his cabin, but it looked pretty well-built. She wondered what would make a man like him move out here by himself. Did he have some tragic history?

Worry pulsed through her at the thought. Maybe that's why he was so brusque? Whatever it was, it shouldn't be taking up space in her head. She'd made two drastic life changes in the past few months, and she needed to figure out who she was from here, not wonder about someone else's issues.

Five

Yep, more people. Women—a whole lot of them, by the sounds of it.

Ian scrubbed a hand through his hair, dislodging a bunch of sawdust, as he walked from the workshop to the cabin. Duke reluctantly trotted by his side. "We're not going down there, Duke," he grumbled. "Let the ladies have their party—it has nothing to do with us."

The women had arrived about an hour ago while Ian was putting in some extra time in the workshop. This month had been busy with orders, with customers wanting to gift furniture items for the holidays. He'd put a hard cap on incoming orders, and now he was booked out until January, since a one-man shop could only produce so much. His specialty was bookcases, end tables, and coffee tables. That kept it simple as well, because he could load the finished pieces into his truck and drive them to the shipping center about an hour outside of Everly Falls.

"What should we have for dinner, huh?"

Duke's tail wagged harder. Sometimes Ian swore the dog understood perfect English.

"How about we heat up a couple of cans of chili, and I'll doctor it with bacon and save a couple of slices for you?"

Duke barked. Ian chuckled and scratched the dog's head, then opened the door to the cabin. Duke normally raced into the house ahead of him, but instead, he turned and bounded down the stairs.

"Hey." Ian pivoted. "Come back!"

Duke ran toward the trees, or more specifically, the path leading through the trees.

"Duke!" he bellowed, and started jogging after him. "Come back. Now!"

Duke ran like a possessed dog, hurtling through the trees. What was up with that? Ian had adopted him from a shelter, and sometimes a completely disobedient side came out if he was triggered by something. And now, Duke was heading straight for . . . Ian groaned. It seemed like the dog was about to crash the women's party.

Ian slowed to a long stride. He wasn't about to jog into Brandy's yard. Up ahead somewhere, Duke barked, and the sound of the women's voices rose as they exclaimed over the sudden appearance of the retriever.

Gritting his teeth, Ian sorted through different scenarios in his mind. He'd apologize, then drag Duke out of there. Maybe he should have brought a dog treat to entice him. No matter. He was nearly to the clearing.

And there was Duke, standing in the middle of the women, who sat in a circle around what looked to be a firepit. Ian didn't remember it being there before, so maybe Brandy had dragged the rocks over? He didn't have time to wonder too much because all four women looked over at him.

Were they friends? Coworkers? He had no idea what

Brandy did for a living.

"Hey, sorry about that." He lifted his hand in a lame attempt at a wave. "Just here to get my dog." He narrowed his gaze at Duke. "Come on, boy, time for your dinner. Leave the ladies to their own dinner."

Each of the women had a plate of food on their laps—looked like grilled kabobs with meat and vegetables. A salad as well. And corn on the cob. Ian tried to remember the last time he'd had corn on the cob. Maybe as a teenager?

"Are you *the neighbor*?" a red-haired woman drawled, pulling Ian from his focus on their plates of delicious-looking food.

"I am." He didn't need to elaborate, did he?

Brandy took over. "Hey, everyone, this is Ian Hudson. Ian, these are my friends—we go way back. Lori, Julie, and Steph."

Steph was the redhead. She rose and crossed to him, extending her hand. Ian shook it and pulled away as soon as it was polite to do so.

"You live up here all by yourself, handsome?" Steph asked.

One of the other women laughed, but Brandy said, "Steph, he doesn't want the third degree."

"I think he's man enough to tell me what he wants." Steph winked as her gaze raked over him.

Ian's throat went dry. The woman was completely ogling him.

"I'm not by myself. I've got Duke," he deadpanned, "and now Brandy is here."

Steph grinned. "I love the name Duke—how'd you come up with it?"

"I, uh . . ." He didn't know where the name came from. "It was his name when I picked him up from the shelter."

"Aww." Steph moved closer and turned to face her friends, setting her hands on her hips. "Did you hear that, ladies? This man adopted a rescue dog."

Brandy's friends fawned even more over Duke. Ian wanted to roll his eyes. Yeah, he thought it was important to adopt pets, but it wasn't like he was an advocate for it.

"Hey." Brandy appeared at Steph's side, appraising him, and he wasn't sure if she was amused, or annoyed that he'd chased his dog into her territory. "Want something to eat? We have plenty."

Again, he couldn't read her tone. It sounded a bit tight. She was probably offering out of politeness. Ian was about to say no, simply because he didn't know how much more of Steph he could take, but his stomach won out. "That's not why I came here."

"I know." Brandy gave him an easy smile, as if they were friends or something. Which they weren't. Acquaintances, sure. What did her smile mean? Because his heart rate had just gone up a notch. "Duke is welcome, too. Can he have chicken?"

"No chicken," Ian said. "I should just take him home to get his dinner."

"What about turkey? I've got some deli meat in the refrigerator."

That, Ian hadn't expected. Maybe Brandy was okay with him being here? She was definitely going the extra mile. Ian's gaze shifted to Duke, who looked like he was in heaven with all the attention from the ladies. "Sure, just a slice or two, though. It will be a treat, but he's on a specific regimen, so I'll feed him his regular dinner later." He was practically blabbering, but he fully blamed that on his growling stomach.

"No problem," Brandy said, her dimple flashing.

Ian released a slow breath. He'd just accepted a dinner invitation from a woman—his neighbor, to be exact—and it was more circumstantial than anything. Another breath. He needed something cold to drink, with tons of ice.

"I'll grab the turkey." Brandy waved toward the fire circle. "Have a seat. I'm sure Steph can make you a plate."

"It would be my pleasure," Steph practically purred.

"Go easy on him," Brandy said to her in an amused tone.

What was going on? Was Steph for real this obnoxious? And why would Brandy want to be friends with someone like that? And why was he staring after Brandy? She was wearing jeans and a navy T-shirt. The most casual he'd seen her yet, although she still wore that pearl necklace from the day before. Her hair was in a ponytail, and it bounced against her shoulders as she walked.

Steph looped her arm through his, and Ian nearly jumped out of his skin.

"Come sit by me, handsome." She didn't wait for an answer, but tugged him along with her.

Would it be rude to shake her off? Thankfully, after he sat, Steph made him a plate, staying busy for a couple of minutes. The other women asked him questions, so he wasn't at Steph's full mercy. He kept his answers short and to the point. Then he turned the tables and asked questions of the women.

"You're all from Everly Falls?"

"Yes, sir," Steph said, returning with his plate. "Been friends since we were kids. Except Julie. She moved in when she was fifteen."

Julie raised a hand, lifting it from her rounded stomach—she looked pregnant. "Yeah, they still consider me the newcomer, even though it's been ten years."

Did that mean Brandy was only twenty-five? Ian was thirty-one, but he felt ancient among these women. Maybe because they didn't look hard and jaded, like he felt inside.

He glanced at the other woman, Lori. Her dark hair was braided into two braids, making her look younger than the others. "Were you all in the same grade?"

"Yep," Steph answered. "How about you, where are you from?"

"Oregon," he said, keeping it vague. "What was it like growing up in a small town?" He'd grown up in a small town, too, but they didn't need to know that. He just wanted to deflect the questions.

Steph answered first, of course, but Ian was hardly paying attention because Brandy came out of the house, a lightness to her step as she carried a paper plate with the turkey slices on it. "Come here, Duke."

Duke didn't need to be asked twice. Apparently, now he decided to be obedient.

"Can I just hand this over, or do you want me to break it into pieces?"

"He's not picky."

Brandy set the plate on the ground, and Duke ate the turkey in about three seconds flat. She hovered over the dog, scratching his back.

Again, she was spoiling the dog, but Ian didn't want to bring it up while they were surrounded by the other women. He should probably stop watching Brandy. He dragged his gaze away from her curved smile, her faint dimple, and her porcelain-blue eyes.

Steph asked him a question, and it took him a moment to figure out what she'd said. The other two women were in their own conversation. "No, I live here year-round."

"Oh, interesting," Steph said. "What do you do all day,

handsome?"

"Work."

She laughed and nudged his arm.

Brandy joined the circle then, Duke faithfully at her side. "Aren't you going to eat, Ian?"

He looked down at his plate. "Yeah."

"Give him a break from the questions, ladies," Brandy said in a teasing tone, but for some reason, Ian heard the pitch of annoyance in her tone. Was she annoyed with him? Or maybe her friends?

He'd quickly eat, then take off. The food was delicious, though. "Who's the chef? This is great."

"We all pitched in," Steph purred next to him. Had she moved her chair closer?

"If you want to stay after sunset, we have s'mores," she added.

"Uh, thanks, but I've got to get back to a few things."

"Like what?" she asked.

"Hey, Julie, did you bring roasting sticks?" Brandy to the rescue, again.

"I think so," Julie said. "I'll check my trunk." She rose and trudged toward one of the parked cars, her hand on her belly.

"Did you build this firepit?" Ian asked, looking at Brandy.

Her eyes filled with amusement. "Yeah, not bad for a city girl, huh?"

He felt a smile push onto his face. "Not bad."

"I'm sure you have some adjustments to make?"

"No, of course not." Ian feigned innocence. He'd finished his food, and as Julie arrived with roasting sticks, he stood. "Thanks so much for the meal. It was great. I should really get Duke fed."

"Sure thing," Brandy said.

Steph was at his side in an instant, her hand resting on his arm. "Stay, Ian. We're just getting to know each other."

It took a lot for Ian to keep the scowl off his face. "Thanks again." He moved away from Steph's touch and focused on Duke. "Come on, boy. We're going home."

A miracle happened. Duke bounded to Ian, then headed toward the trail through the trees. He waved a hand at the women, then followed Duke. He was tempted to break into a jog, but he willed his feet to keep to a steady pace, though he couldn't will the slowing of his heart rate until long after he'd reached his cabin.

Six

THE LIGHTS FROM IAN'S CABIN winked through the trees even though it was after ten o'clock. So he must be awake, right? Besides, Brandy didn't have his cell number, so knocking on his door was really the only way she could directly speak to him. And she didn't want to wait until the next day, because the needed apology kept plaguing her.

She'd forgotten how Steph could be around guys. It had been a long time since a girls' night had included anyone from the male species. Usually, they met at one another's houses, ate potluck, and gabbed the night away. Steph always had adventurous dating stories that made everyone laugh. But they'd never had an actual man in their mix.

Of course, Ian appearing with his dog had been unexpected. But it was like Steph had rehearsed pickup lines that were way over-the-top flirty.

Brandy had tried to deflect Steph's behavior with humor, but truthfully, it had really bothered her, and it still bothered her. Ian Hudson was a man who could hold his own, so that wasn't the problem. Brandy felt guilty since she was the hostess and *her* friend had misbehaved toward their guest—even though he'd been a last-minute addition. She knew he'd been about to turn down the dinner invite, and she wasn't surprised he'd turned down the s'mores roast.

She'd been curious to hear Ian's answers to Steph's persistent questions, but Brandy had also noticed how he kept deflecting the focus away from himself. Impressive, really. Brock would have talked the entire time about himself if given the chance.

So now, here she was, approaching the steps that led to his cabin door. Would the dog bark when he sensed her presence? So far, all was quiet. No sound of music or a television or anything.

She walked up the stairs, drew in a deep breath, then slowly released it. She knocked on the door, hoping it wasn't too loud, or too soft, and waited a few heartbeats, then decided she'd made a mistake. She could see Ian tomorrow or another day. Their paths would certainly cross at some point in the near future.

Yeah, that's what she'd do. Wait.

She headed down the steps, keeping her footsteps as silent as possible.

"Brandy?"

She turned at the sound of his voice. She hadn't even heard the door open. Ian stood in the doorway, with Duke trying to press between his leg and the door frame. He was barefoot, wearing jeans and a T-shirt, his usual outfit. Did he not dress down at night?

"Hi, I didn't mean to bother you." Brandy gripped her hands together. "I just wanted to apologize for earlier."

Ian's brow furrowed, and he stepped out onto the porch, closing the door between him and the dog. On the other side of the door, Duke gave a whine of protest. "Apologize for what?"

"My friend, Steph."

Ian's expression cleared. "Ah. She's, uh, interesting."

"Yeah, that's one way to put it. I didn't realize that was how she'd act—around you or any man. I mean, she was like that in high school, but every teenager is kind of zany that way. Usually our get-togethers are women only. So I guess I was surprised, but mostly embarrassed."

"It wasn't your fault." Ian folded his arms and leaned against the door frame, ignoring Duke's whining on the other side of the door. "You shouldn't have to apologize for another person's behavior. Besides, the food was delicious, and Duke was in heaven with all the attention."

Well, then. Her grumpy neighbor had just turned a little bit sweet.

"Duke *was* in heaven." She smiled.

And Ian smiled back. Which made butterflies appear in her stomach without her permission.

"I don't mind saying hi to Duke—he sounds like he's in a lot of distress right now."

Ian laughed. And now she knew the man could laugh. The low rumble only made the butterflies in her stomach fly faster.

"All right." Ian opened the door, and Duke bounded out, heading straight for Brandy.

She squealed when the dog nearly ran into her.

"Chill, Duke, and don't jump."

Brandy bent over and scratched the sides of the dog's head with both hands. "He's a sweetheart."

"Duke . . ." Ian warned.

"I don't mind, really." Brandy glanced up at Ian. "I love how happiness just exudes from him. He's so easy to please."

"Yeah, but not everyone wants a dog acting hyper around them."

"I'm sure he'll mellow when he's used to me." Oops, what had she said? Brandy tried to think of a save as she scrubbed Duke's belly because he'd slunk to the ground and rolled over. "I mean, not that we're going to be hanging out or anything. I just mean that the newness will wear off."

Ian hadn't answered, and she peeked up at him. He'd moved to the top of the stairs, one hand braced on the railing, his green eyes on her. They were unreadable from Brandy's position.

"So, Duke's from a shelter?" she said lamely. "How long have you had him?"

"About two-and-a-half years." Ian lowered himself to the top step. "His owner had a ranch, so Duke ran wild most of the time. It's harder to train an adult dog than a puppy, but he's doing pretty well. With the exception of crashing your party."

"Oh, it was totally fine." Brandy moved to one of the lower steps and sat down. Duke stuck to her like glue, so she continued to scratch his head as the dog leaned against her legs. "I haven't seen my friends for a few weeks, so it was kind of like a mini reunion."

"A *few weeks*?" Ian said. "You must all be really close if that's a long time not to see each other."

Brandy gave a little shrug. "Yeah, we're close, but we only get together about once a month. We'd just cross paths a lot in town—you know, small town and all."

Ian rested his elbows on his knees and laced his hands together. "Yeah, I know. I grew up in a small town in southern Oregon."

"Oh." Brandy was grateful for the distraction of the dog, because sitting only a couple of feet from Ian was making her aware of a lot of little things about him. How his muscular forearms rested on his knees. The scar across his knuckle—

white against his olive skin. His nails were short and clean, and his hair wasn't peppered in sawdust at the moment. She'd been curious about that. Both times he'd showed up at her cottage, he'd looked like he'd walked off of a construction site. But now, he was all cleaned up. And . . . smelled of spicy soap.

She looked back at Duke. "Big family?"

"Just me and my dad."

It was a strange thing to be having such a personal conversation with Ian Hudson. His standoffishness from the previous day seemed to have faded. But she also sensed he was intensely private, and his general grumpiness was to maintain that. Now that she knew he didn't have a mother in his life—for who knew how long—she felt like she'd gained another insight about him. Not that gaining insights into Ian had been her goal in coming over tonight.

"What about you?" he asked, his voice low, mellow.

"One sister—Everly—who you met. And my mom—who you'll meet. My dad died years ago."

"Sorry about your dad." His statement was an echo of something she'd heard over and over in her life, but Ian's tone was sincere. As if he knew the pain of loss, which she assumed he did with no mother in his life.

She nodded and slowly stroked one of Duke's soft ears. His eyes were closed, and she wondered if a dog could fall asleep half sitting, half leaning.

"Do you always wear pearls?"

Brandy's hand went automatically to her throat. "Most days. They're from my dad—well, they were his mom's. And he gave them to me as a kid and told me I could start wearing them when I was eighteen, which I did."

"They suit you," Ian said in a soft voice.

Something deep inside of her warmed. Before she could

analyze that, he asked, "Why am I meeting your mom?"

Brandy looked up again. "Because when she comes up here tomorrow to complain in person about my dilapidated circumstances, she'll knock on your door and introduce herself. Consider this your warning."

Ian's brow tugged down. "Does she do that to all your neighbors?"

"Nope. This will be a first." Brandy gave a small, nervous smile. "But I haven't lived in the middle of nowhere before, and she thinks I'm having a midlife crisis at twenty-five."

Ian didn't smile back. In fact, his green eyes had turned more serious. "Are you dealing with a crisis?"

Brandy pushed out a breath. Just thinking about Brock, let alone talking about him, made her stomach feel sour. Why had she even said anything? She should have kept her mom's arrival a surprise. "Three months ago, I was supposed to get married." Her voice cut off because her throat suddenly went tight.

She felt Ian's gaze on her.

"And you didn't?" he asked in a quiet voice.

"No," she whispered. Dang it. Her eyes were burning with tears—tears that should have been shed already. Where were they coming from?

"Do you want a drink or anything? Water? Juice? Wine? Or something stronger?"

Brandy wiped at her eyes, probably smearing the faded remnants of her mascara. "No, I'm fine. I should get back. It's been a long couple of days—months, really. And I came here to apologize, not force you to be neighborly."

She pushed up off the stairs. Duke shot to his feet, suddenly alert. Brandy scratched his head a final time. "Good night, Duke." Then she looked over at Ian. He'd risen to his feet, too, his hands shoved in his front pockets.

"I'll walk you back."

"You don't have to."

"I'll follow you, then, at a distance."

Brandy released a sigh. She couldn't read his expression. Was he annoyed that she'd cut into his nighttime routine—whatever that was? She headed toward the path, Ian's footsteps behind her. This time, though, she didn't start to jog. They didn't exactly walk side by side, but he was only a pace behind her. Duke trotted up ahead, as if he were the leader of his own pack.

The moon and stars were bright enough that Brandy didn't worry about tripping on something. Ian didn't speak, didn't ask her questions about her tale of woe, and she was grateful for that. Her throat still burned with emotion, and she knew more tears would be easily triggered. When she reached the clearing, she turned.

Ian had stopped by the line of trees, Duke at his side.

"Thanks again for being gracious about Steph." She gave him a faint smile. "And for following me home."

He nodded. "No problem."

Well, that was that. She turned again and headed toward her place. When Ian spoke again, she paused.

"Brandy, if you need anything, you're welcome to knock on my door. Anytime."

She drew in a sharp breath. She liked the way her name sounded when he said it. The butterflies were back despite the mess that was her head and heart. "That's a very neighborly offer."

She wished she could read his eyes, but it was too dark, and she was too far away. But his response made her smile. "Forget what I said yesterday."

"Everything?" she teased in a quiet voice.

His chuckle was soft against the quiet night. "I don't remember everything I said, but yeah."

"It's a deal. If you can forget about Steph, I can forget a few things, too."

He nodded again. "Good night, Brandy."

Her voice caught in her throat, but she managed to say, "Good night, Ian."

Seven

ALTHOUGH IAN WAS IN HIS workshop, staining a bookcase, he could hear someone knocking on the front door of his cabin. He'd left the windows open, but shut the workshop door since he didn't want Duke heading to Brandy's when he heard the arrival of her mom. Ian knew it was only a matter of time before Mrs. Kane came to meet him. Brandy *had* warned him.

Ian set down the paintbrush and removed his work apron. Then he wiped his hands on a towel he kept on one of the tables, although it didn't do much good. Duke was already at the door of the workshop, tail wagging fiercely.

"You're staying here, bud," he told the dog. "Don't want you jumping all over an older woman."

But when Ian walked out of the workshop, the woman on his porch didn't look much older than Brandy. She turned to face him fully.

"Oh, there you are," Mrs. Kane said in a singsong voice. "I hope I'm not interrupting anything."

"It's fine." Ian tried to keep his voice conciliatory.

Mrs. Kane came down the steps, her high heels wobbling a bit. He thought Brandy had dressed too fancy for cabin life, but her mother looked like she was going to a luncheon with the governor.

"I'm Lydia Kane," she said the moment her heels hit the bottom step.

By then, Ian had crossed the grassy area.

Her eyes were a darker blue than her daughter's, and they were assessing him from head to foot. She wore a pantsuit of pale peach, along with a blue-and-peach scarf tied about her neck. Her lips pursed as her gaze met his once again. "You must be Ian Hudson."

"I am." He held out his hand, and she shook it quite firmly. He wasn't surprised.

"Did you build this place?" She turned to survey the cabin.

He should be annoyed, but he was only amused. This woman was as direct with her questions as he was. "I hired the people who built it, if that's what you mean."

Mrs. Kane cast him a side-eyed glance, her lips quirking. "It's a beautiful cabin. Maybe next time you can give me the tour, but today I'm out of time." She faced him, folding her arms.

Ian decided she looked like an older version of Brandy, though her short-bobbed blonde hair was intermixed with silver strands. Her blue gaze studied his face. Could she read minds or something?

"Look, Ian—can I call you Ian?"

He hesitated. Did he need to give her permission? "Of course."

Mrs. Kane flashed a quick smile, then she patted his arm. "Great. Call me Lydia. Now that we're acquainted with each other, we can get on the same page."

What was she talking about?

Mrs. Kane, er, Lydia, dropped her voice. "Brandy is going through a really tough time, and I worry about her secluding herself from everything and everyone." Her brows pulled together. "It's not her personality to do this. I mean, I understand she needed to get away for a short time, but it's time to face reality. Brock will always be in Everly Falls, so she can't avoid him forever. Might as well face everything head-on, so she can continue her life as it used to be and not let her ex-fiancé control her behavior and actions."

Ah, *Brock* was the name of the ex. Ian didn't know why he was being made privy to all of this information. Did Lydia Kane go around to everyone in Everly Falls and spill details about her daughter's life?

"So I need your help."

Ian's eyes about popped. "With what?"

Lydia adjusted the scarf about her neck. "Encourage her to return to Everly Falls. Whenever you see her, just drop in something nice about the town. You know, to remind her what she's missing out on."

Ian cleared his throat. He couldn't think of one thing Brandy was missing out on by living up here. "I don't know if I'm the right person for the job. Besides, I don't like the idea of trying to influence your daughter to change her mind about something that she probably carefully considered."

Lydia stared at him for a long moment. "Huh. Well, I guess we'll agree to disagree." Her gaze shifted, and she pointed toward the workshop. "What's in that building?"

"My workshop." He didn't elaborate, so he wasn't surprised when Lydia continued.

"And what does a man like you do in a workshop all the way up here?" She wrinkled her nose as she looked around.

He could hear Duke whining to be let out. "Come and

look around," Ian said. "And you can meet my dog, Duke."

He wasn't sure where this very neighborly invitation had come from, but it was too late to take it back now because Lydia Kane was walking with him toward the workshop.

"Duke, sit," he commanded through the door before cracking it open. Two soulful brown eyes met his gaze. "Sit, boy. We have a visitor."

Duke sat, his tail thumping, his mouth open as he panted.

Ian opened the door wider and stepped in first, putting himself between the dog and Lydia.

"Oh." Lydia entered next and stopped a few feet from the door as she looked around.

Ian tried to see the workshop through her eyes. The sections of unfinished wood propped against the far wall. The long table with various saws and sanders. The smaller table filled with paint cans and stains. And the row of finished or half-finished furniture.

"You're a carpenter?"

"Yes."

Lydia crossed to the bookcase that he'd been staining.

"It's still wet," he said.

She stopped a couple of feet short, then leaned forward, examining it closer. "You've matched the grain at the jointures."

"Yes." He was surprised she'd noticed, but not much seemed to get past this woman.

Lydia straightened, then looked over at him. "I thought you were some software company mogul. That's what Everly told me."

"I sold my company." Short and sweet. He didn't want to get into any of that. "And this is my hobby turned business."

Lydia's gaze shifted to the rest of the room again. A minute passed, then two. Apparently, she was speechless?

"Thanks for showing me the workshop."

"No problem."

She crossed to the door again, skirted Duke, and walked outside.

Ian rubbed at the back of his neck, then stepped outside, too. Duke was still sitting, watching, obviously having decided that Lydia wasn't a person to lavish him with affection like her daughter had.

She turned to face him, a hand on her hip. "Even if you don't agree with me, I'd appreciate your cooperation about Brandy."

"I don't—"

"We'll be in touch." Lydia turned and walked toward the road, her heels wobbling. Should he tell her about the shortcut through the trees?

She pulled out her phone and called someone. The last thing Ian heard was her saying, "Everly, I've met him . . ."

Ian didn't know whether to laugh or to lock all of his doors, or maybe sell the property and find another place to live. His quiet, peaceful life had now been infiltrated. Brandy was fine, though. And when she didn't have guests over, things were very quiet. He wasn't sure what she did all day, but she kept to herself.

Ian didn't know how long he stayed outside the workshop, staring at the trees as thoughts churned in his mind, but it was long enough to hear a car engine start up and tires spin away on the dirt road. Had Brandy left with her mom? Whatever was happening, he shouldn't be dwelling on it.

"Come on, Duke, back to work." He'd be taking a load of furniture to the shipping center tomorrow, and this was the last layer of stain for the bookcase.

A text buzzed his phone as he crossed the shop floor. Ian fished his phone out of his back pocket. Not a lot of people texted him anymore. People from his old life had slowly dropped off, one by one. The furniture orders came through his website, and he dealt with customers through email.

Ian froze when he saw the name on the text: *Pete.*

His former business partner and stealer of his wife. The first few words were visible, and Ian's vision clouded when he saw Ella's name. What was all this about? If he opened the text, Pete would see that it had been read. Was it a wedding announcement or something? Ian released a bitter laugh. He didn't need to know anything more about their relationship, or their lives for that matter.

Finally, he decided that not knowing what the text said would bug him until he read it. So with a sigh, he opened the text and read: *Hey, just wanted to give you a heads-up about Ella. Her mom died yesterday and the funeral is tomorrow afternoon in San Diego. It was planned already because of the cancer. Ella would never tell you to come, but I know she'd like you there since you were close to her mom. Here's the address and time . . .*

Ian's pulse pounded so hard in his head that he had trouble focusing on the rest of the message. That was the thing about divorce, or breakups in general. You didn't just marry one person, you married the entire family. Their family became your family, and Ella's mom Valerie had become his mom.

Ian's eyes slid shut. He'd known about the cancer. She'd beat it three years ago and had gone into remission. It must have returned with a vengeance. Valerie's smiling face popped into his mind. She'd been a quiet, unassuming woman. Salt of the earth. Mellow personality. Which was just what Ian needed at the time in a mother-in-law. His own mother had ditched his dad when Ian was three years old, so he had no memories of her. Just knew the pain it had caused his dad.

Ian's own pain would come later in elementary school when all the other kids had moms coming to school events and performances. When Ian was sixteen, his dad informed him that his mother had died. And any hope he'd had of ever being reunited with his mom again had died that day, too. Until Valerie. She'd been an unexpected silver lining in his life when he married Ella. Sometimes he thought the most painful part of the divorce, after the betrayal, was losing Valerie as a mother-in-law, even though she told him he could reach out to her anytime. He had just been too stubborn and found it was easier just to cut himself off from everything and everyone. At a remote cabin.

And now . . . it had all changed again.

"Ian?" A woman's voice cut into his distressing thoughts.

He looked over at the open doorway, where Brandy stood, petting a very happy Duke. He wiped at the tears that burned his eyes. There was no use hiding them because Brandy was looking right at him.

"Are you . . . okay? Was my mother that horrible?"

Ian crossed to the table and took a swig from a water bottle. "Your mom was fine," he rasped. "I . . . just got some bad news, that's all."

Brandy's brow crinkled, and she straightened from Duke. "Oh, I'm so sorry. Is there anything I can do or help with?"

He puffed out a breath and closed his eyes. "No, nothing. It's just . . ." He opened his eyes and looked toward the windows and the pine trees beyond. Everything was so remote out here, so far away from all that he used to be involved with. Why was news about Valerie such a blow? Maybe because he didn't know the cancer was back. And maybe because Valerie had been the one decent thing in his life for so long—even though they hadn't talked in months.

Footsteps sounded, and Brandy walked closer.

"How about I bring over some dinner later? My mom brought tons of groceries, and I'll never be able to eat everything before it all spoils. I'll drop it off on your porch around six?"

Her words were soft, and Ian wished he could respond appropriately, but his throat had tightened. He could only nod as he blinked back more tears.

Without another word, Brandy walked out of the workshop, leaving him to his memories.

Eight

As Brandy stirred the taco soup on the stove, her heart ached for Ian even though she didn't know why he was so upset. It wasn't often she came across a grown man with tears in his eyes. She'd panicked at first, wondering if her mother had said or done something—though that seemed unrealistic. So what had happened? She knew very little about Ian Hudson, of course, which made the possibilities seem endless.

It wasn't really any of her business anyway, and if she hadn't happened to walk into his workshop at that very moment, she wouldn't even know something was going on. She'd also been very curious about the carpentry work he did. Her mother had told her all about it, of course—and how it was high-quality handmade work. According to Everly, Ian had sold out of a successful software company. So was carpentry his new career? The mysteries about the man just kept piling up.

Brandy pushed back all the questions, then turned off the element. She used a mug to ladle several portions of the taco soup into a large bowl with a lid. Then she packed up tortilla chips, sour cream, and grated cheese. Next, she grabbed the plate of brownies she'd made earlier. She placed everything into a grocery box to carry to Ian's. It was nearly six, and the sun was setting, bringing on the coolness of the evening.

As she walked along the path to Ian's cabin, she thought of other things her mother had said about the man. *He's very mysterious. But he seems to have a stubborn personality.*

Brandy had smiled through all of the assessments. She hadn't known about the carpentry work, but it made sense. He was frequently covered in sawdust. She'd wondered if he was just working on things for his cabin, but when she walked into the workshop earlier in the day, it was clear he was running some sort of business. Interesting. That kind of labor also explained why his physique was so, um, sculpted.

She really shouldn't let her mind go there. Attraction to a man was not on the table for her right now. Maybe in the future—the *far distant* future.

When she came out of the trees and approached the cabin, she didn't expect to see the door wide open. Music came from inside, not loud, but definitely with a thumping beat. Duke was lying on the porch, and the second he spotted her, he jumped up and ran toward her.

"Hey, Duke, my hands are full. Where's Ian?"

The dog let out a merry bark and followed her up the steps to the front door. She couldn't very well leave the food on the porch if Duke was there, too. The dog would probably help himself.

She stopped at the open doorway and stared. The cabin was gorgeous inside. Wood beams framed the walls and ceiling. The leather furniture of the front room looked cozy and welcoming. A pale blue rug stretched across the floor.

And beyond the front room, she could see part of a kitchen that looked like it had been built for a gourmet chef.

"Ian?" she called. She couldn't see him, and the music seemed to be coming from a back room. She could maybe come back later, since she'd never ended up getting his number.

"Duke, go get Ian," she said at last.

The dog seemed to understand her—at least she thought he did, because he ran down the hallway that probably led to the bedrooms? A door shut somewhere inside the cabin, then the music switched off, and suddenly, Ian appeared in the hallway. Wearing only a towel.

She knew she was blushing—not because she hadn't ever seen a man in a towel, but because she felt like an intruder. Or maybe she was blushing because Ian Hudson was a fine specimen of a human. Maybe he lifted weights, too? Did he have a weight room in his pristine cabin?

"Hey," Brandy said over the zooming of her pulse. "Brought you dinner. Your door was open, and I didn't want to leave it on the porch."

"Is it six already?"

He was walking toward her, completely oblivious to his undressed state.

"I'm, uh, a little early." Like ten minutes.

"Ah." He reached her and took the box, peering inside. "Looks amazing. Thank you."

Brandy tried not to inhale, but she had to breathe, right? And Ian smelled like freshly showered man. She averted her gaze from his torso and chest and shoulders and pretty much any expanse of flesh. His face—that was a safe place to look.

Maybe not.

His green eyes were bright with amusement when he lifted his gaze from the box. "Are you checking me out?"

Brandy almost swallowed her tongue. "No. I'm . . . um . . ."

"I'll go get dressed," he said, a knowing smile on his face. "Come in. Duke must have opened the door—he'll do that if I don't lock it."

Brandy didn't know what to respond to first because Ian was walking toward the kitchen. He set the box on the counter, then looked over at her. "I thought maybe we could share the meal? Is there enough for two?"

Somehow, Brandy got her words out. "More than enough."

"Great, just give me a couple of minutes." He headed down the hall again and disappeared.

Brandy didn't move for a second. Her mind whirled. She *had* been checking out Ian Hudson—well, who could blame her? He'd walked right up to her wearing only a towel. Any woman in the world would have ogled him a bit. Then he'd invited her inside and asked her to eat with him.

Maybe she should just leave. She didn't want Ian to think she was checking him out, whether he was half-dressed or not. But then again, he'd had actual tears in his eyes earlier. He was going through something hard, so maybe she could just be a friend, or simply company right now?

He didn't have those tears when he took the box from her. So that was good, she decided. Maybe the news hadn't been that bad and he was just a crier?

She scoffed at herself. Somehow, she knew that Ian wasn't the overly sentimental type. Whatever he'd been sad over was something tragic.

All right, then, Brandy. Be a good neighbor.

She closed the door, then headed toward the kitchen. Duke trotted after her and sat by the table, watching everything Brandy was doing. She unpacked the items she'd packed up only moments before.

She didn't know where to look for bowls or spoons, so she started opening cupboards. The third cupboard had the dishes. Plates lined the lower shelf, then smaller plates sat on the next shelf up. On the third, higher shelf, were the bowls.

Pushing up on her toes, she reached for a couple of bowls.

"I've got it," Ian said, his voice rumbling next to her. He easily reached above her and took down the bowls.

His clean shower scent filled her senses again, and she stepped away from him, if only to clear her mind.

"Thanks," she squeaked.

Ian's gaze landed on hers. "Thank *you*. It smells delicious."

"Yeah . . ." She was staring at him. His dark hair was still damp, and he'd pulled on a black T-shirt and faded jeans. He was barefoot again. She didn't know why she liked him barefoot. Maybe because his boots were so loud? Or maybe because he seemed less brusque when he was dressed down a little? He definitely wasn't brusque right now. "It's pretty easy to make—one of my go-to meals."

"*Easy* has never been in my cooking vocabulary." Ian's attention moved to the food on the table. "I mostly warm up food from a can."

"Cans are good in a pinch."

His chuckle was low. "That's one way to put it." He pulled out two glasses from another cupboard, then filled them up with water from the fridge. Next, he walked toward the table and cracked open the lid. His kitchen filled with the smell of taco soup. He leaned down and inhaled. "I'm starving."

Brandy smiled, then realized she was watching his every

movement. She blinked and straightened. "Well, let's eat, then. Fill up a bowl, then put on whatever toppings you want."

"Wait, what's this?" He picked up the plate of brownies.

"Brownies."

His brows quirked, almost comically. "You made dessert?"

"Yeah, brownies from a box—super easy."

Ian's gaze scanned her, and the edges of his mouth lifted. "There's that *easy* word again."

Brandy wasn't going to get all hot again, so she attempted a casual smile. "Eat up, Mr. Hudson. Soup's getting cold."

"Yes, ma'am."

She smirked, ignoring the butterflies that zoomed about her stomach. This man certainly appreciated his food, which had nothing to do with her personally. She could also see how he'd be so appreciative if he really only cooked from cans. It wasn't like he could order food delivered all the way up here—delivery fees would be a fortune.

After they both sat down with their bowls, Ian dug in immediately. After the first bite, he closed his eyes. When he opened them again, he said, "I don't think I've had real homemade food since . . . well, since I was a teenager living at home and my dad and I were invited to a neighbor's barbecue."

Brandy stared at him. "Are you serious?"

"Yeah." Ian shrugged and took another bite. "Not even my wife cooked."

Brandy nearly dropped her spoon. Ian had a *wife*? Where was she? Were they separated?

Ian must have felt her incredulous gaze, because he looked up. "My ex-wife, that is."

Ah, that made sense. "Sorry."

He was still looking at her. "Sorry that I'm divorced or that I've been deprived of homemade cooking?"

"Both?" Her mind raced with this new information about him. She was very glad he wasn't married—that would have made this private meal extremely awkward. She scrambled for something to say. "I assume you read, though, and can follow a recipe? Honestly, basic cooking isn't that hard. Baking can be tricky if you're making something that involves yeast and rising times, or glazing, or whipping stuff into peaks. But a box of brownies is really simple, just takes reading the back of a box, three eggs, a half cup of oil, a cup of water, the mix, and a whisk."

Ian blinked. "I have no idea what you said."

She had been totally rambling. Drawing in a breath, she said, "If you want, I can teach you a few basics."

Ian scanned her face, and Brandy wondered about all the scrutiny. What was going on in that head of his?

"Maybe," he finally said.

"Maybe?"

"Well, I don't want to take advantage of your time." He reached for his glass of water and took a drink. "Besides, that would be *extremely* neighborly."

"Yeah, you're right," Brandy amended in a teasing voice. "That would definitely be very neighborly."

Ian gave a small shake of his head, but a smile played on his lips before he took another bite of his soup. "I hope you're not hungry, because I could eat the entire thing."

For some reason, this made her very pleased. "Eat as much as you want. I have more at the cottage."

Ian's eyes flashed at her with appreciation, then he continued eating. When he was filling up a second helping, he said in a matter-of-fact voice, "My ex-mother-in-law died this week. I barely found out when you came into the workshop."

"Oh." Brandy blinked. "I'm so sorry. How old was she?"

"Only sixty," he said. "She had breast cancer a few years ago, but beat it. It came back, I guess—I didn't know that, either, until today. I haven't talked to Valerie since the divorce proceedings with Ella. Ironically, Valerie lives, or lived, in San Diego—so only a few hours away. Much closer than when I was married to her daughter and living in Northern California. I assume Ella told her mom not to contact me, but I never reached out, either. Now I regret that. Valerie was an amazing woman."

"I'm really sorry," Brandy said.

Ian's tone was somber, but he wasn't tearing up again. "I am, too. And now I'm in a dilemma. The funeral is tomorrow afternoon. I want to go, but I don't know if the memories it will dredge up will throw me for a loop. Make me even more of a recluse." He smiled when he said it, but Brandy wasn't fooled.

There was deep pain in those green eyes of his. She hadn't fully connected all that he'd told her, but she was beginning to see a bigger picture of why he lived in the hills by himself. Obviously, the divorce from Ella had led him to make drastic changes in his life. Which Brandy completely understood. She was living up here, too, keeping away from her previous life.

"Maybe it will be closure?" she suggested. "In a good way?"

Ian nodded at this, seeming to consider. "Maybe."

Nine

WOULD ATTENDING VALERIE'S FUNERAL BE closure? Ian wondered. Heaven knew he needed that. He was tired of the ache in his gut every time something reminded him of his ex-wife, or his ex-best friend Pete, or their company. Which happened every day.

Brandy had turned her attention to Duke, who was more than happy to receive it. She was finished eating, apparently, and he watched her. She wasn't all gussied up like the other times he'd seen her. Instead, she wore cut-off shorts, sandals, and a light-pink T-shirt with the word "GROOVY" scrawled across her chest in red. Her very blonde hair was scooped into a ponytail, which showed off the pearls she always wore. She must have scrubbed her face clean, because there wasn't any makeup to conceal the dusting of freckles across her nose and cheeks.

Brandy was beautiful without all the trappings of makeup and coordinating outfits. Well, she was beautiful either way, but Ian could appreciate this comfortable version. He probably shouldn't be analyzing his neighbor so much, but his brain seemed to have a mind of its own.

Ian ate the last few bites of his second helping of the taco soup. He still had yet to find out much about Brandy, but the conversation with her mom had been enlightening on some things. What would she do if he brought it up? Would she be upset at her mom?

"If I go, I should probably let Ella know I'm coming." Ian set his spoon down. "We haven't had any communication for months, and I don't want my arrival to trigger negative stuff. At least on her end."

"Will it trigger negative stuff for you?" Brandy lifted her gaze to meet his, her blue eyes more azure in the kitchen lighting. "Was the divorce terrible? I mean, I'm sure it was . . . All divorces are terrible, I'm sure. Sorry, I'm being a busybody like my mom."

Her cheeks had pinked.

"It's fine." He wasn't bothered by her questions, although he hadn't talked to anyone about his divorce. His father was gone, and it wasn't like he could discuss it with Valerie. His former friends had faded off when he ditched his company. "At first, it was rough. It all feels so long ago now, so that text from Pete jolted a lot of memories I'd forgotten. Or at least tried to forget."

"Pete? Is that Ella's brother or father?"

"Uh, no." Ian stood and cleared the table, carrying the bowls and spoons to the sink. He turned on the water and began to wash everything out.

"I can help." Brandy appeared next to him, carrying the water glasses.

He looked over at her. "You cooked, so the least I can do is wash dishes."

She didn't move, though. Instead, she snatched the kitchen towel hanging from the oven handle and began to dry the dishes after he washed them.

They worked in silence for a few moments. Ian didn't feel pressured to explain things to Brandy, yet it was kind of nice to share with her. When he'd finished washing, he grabbed another kitchen towel, and together they finished all the drying.

Ian leaned against the counter and folded his arms. "Pete Callahan was my business partner. We go way back to high school, and we also attended the same university. When we created a data storage company together, we had no idea how successful it would be. We took it public three years ago."

Brandy leaned against the counter a few feet from him, listening.

"Ella was, and is, a brilliant software engineer," he continued. "We hit it off almost immediately, but we kept things casual for months, because you know—employee-boss relationships. Pete suspected, though, and didn't seem to have a problem with us. So we dated for real and ended up marrying."

He paused and looked toward the darkened windows. "I don't know when it all began—and I don't really want to know—but Ella and Pete started their own relationship."

"Oh wow," Brandy said, her tone sympathetic. "I'm so sorry, Ian. I haven't been married, but I understand the betrayal..."

He met her gaze, feeling her sincerity. "Ella didn't want to go to marriage counseling or try to reconcile anything between us. I guess I was the fool for not knowing my own wife had fallen in love with someone else. Or maybe she'd never loved me."

"Oh, Ian," Brandy whispered, resting a hand on his arm. "That's awful. I can't even imagine how hard that was."

The simple touch was somehow comforting, and the

shared meal had been nice, too. He felt less alone right now, less broken and messed up in the head. "It's all in the past. I haven't replied to Pete's text yet. As you can see, it's complicated."

Brandy dropped her hand. "Yeah, really complicated. I get it, though. My relationship with my ex-fiancé was really complicated, too."

Ian moved to the table and sat down. Duke leaned against his leg, as if he were trying to offer some comfort, too. He patted the dog. "Complicated how?"

Brandy bit her lip, as if she were debating.

"Never mind, it's none of my business," Ian said. "Your mom did tell me that your ex's name is Brock."

Brandy grimaced. "She told you that, huh?"

"Among other things."

She crossed to the table, taking the seat across from him. He decided that he liked Brandy in his kitchen—it felt comfortable. He hadn't realized he'd missed talking in-person with someone until now.

"What other things?" she asked.

It wasn't like he was loyal to Lydia Kane, and besides, he wasn't about to go along with the woman's plans anyway. Brandy should know about her mom's persistence if she didn't already. "Your mom wants me to convince you to move back into the valley. You know, resume your old life, which includes getting past your canceled wedding."

Brandy wrinkled her nose. "I don't know whether I should apologize for my mom or laugh at the image of her trying to get *you* on her side. The innocent neighbor who didn't know I existed last week."

"No apologies needed, remember?" Ian rested his arms on the table. "You don't need to apologize for other people."

Brandy's smile appeared, her single dimple appearing.

"Noted."

"I am curious, though, about why things were so complicated with your ex." Ian dragged the plate of brownies toward him. "But you don't need to tell me if you don't want to."

Brandy's eyes stayed on his movements as he removed the cellophane wrap from the plate and offered her a brownie. She took one and bit into it.

Ian followed suit. "Delicious. Thanks again, Brandy."

"You're welcome." She took another bite of hers. "Hmm. So Brock Hayes dated my sister before he met me."

Ian lowered his brownie. "What?"

"Yeah, I'm sure you can guess where this is all going." Her eyes filled with amusement. "Brock and Everly dated a few months while I was in college. When I came home after graduating, everything went haywire. I felt an instant connection to Brock—and he showered me with attention. He broke up with my sister, and the next thing I knew, he asked me out, claiming they'd been casual—all that stuff. I didn't know what to think at first, so I called Everly. She told me she'd noticed the connection and that it was kind of awkward for her, but she'd never stand in the way if Brock and I were meant to be."

Ian could only stare at her. "So it was *meant to be*? You got engaged?"

"Yeah." Brandy's cheeks pinked as she looked down at the table. She traced the grain of the wood with one finger. "I thought he was the one . . . I really did. He was charming, sweet, always giving me flowers, wanted to be with me every moment I had free, made friends with all my friends. He agreed with everything I said, and we had tons of things in common—at first. He took a cooking class so we could cook together, and every night, we'd cook dinner. We'd even grocery shop together. In fact, he'd get upset if I did things without him. I thought it was cute—at first."

Ian didn't like any of this—all he saw were red flags of a possessive boyfriend. "He love-bombed you."

Brandy looked up, her gaze sharp. "What?"

"You know, he came into your life and took over, but made it seem like it was romance."

She opened her mouth, then closed it. "Yeah . . . that makes sense, but I thought love-bombing was what narcissists do." Her eyes widened. "Oh my gosh."

"The signs are there . . ." he said quietly.

She blinked, and her eyes filled with tears. "How could I be so stupid?"

Ian reached for her hand. "You're not stupid. I only know this because Ella was the same way. She doted on me, at least at first. Further into our relationship, whenever I had an issue with something, she turned it around so I was the one who ended up apologizing."

Brandy nodded. "That's how it was with Brock. He paid me tons of attention, but things were really about *him*. He took everything to the extreme—working out at the gym and going on hunting trips in Africa. I mean, I get hunting for animals that people actually use and eat, but trophy hunting is a different story. Especially when you can't really afford it."

"Yeah, Pete got into that for a while, but he could afford it," Ian said. "I never caught the bug."

"That might be a good thing." Lines appeared between her brows. "He started collecting rifles, and I didn't think much of it since they were all for hunting, but then he bought a pistol. When I told him I didn't grow up in a house with handguns, and I was a bit nervous about him having one, he made it sound like he'd bought it to protect *me*. But he kept buying them, and I lost track of what he had once he filled two safes."

"Huh. He sounds like a serious collector."

"I don't know about that—it was like he'd go from one obsession to another. Guns just became that next fad for him."

"I own a pistol," Ian said in a quiet voice. "Most people in a large city have them, and that's where I lived for so long, but I don't open carry."

"That makes more sense." Brandy exhaled. "His latest obsession was joining boards of charity organizations that do humanitarian work in Africa. He thought if he was on the board, that would be another stream of income for *him*. Still, I talked myself out of my worries over and over. Always giving him the benefit of the doubt. Until my sister Everly showed up at a family brunch with her new boyfriend, Austin. You met him the other day . . ."

He nodded for her to continue.

"Brock claims he got confused and old feelings arose. He called Everly and told her that he missed her and still had feelings for her. She wasn't supposed to tell me about the phone call."

"Whoa," was all Ian could say. He couldn't imagine two sisters enduring such a situation.

"Everly called me and told me everything." Brandy wiped at her eyes. "I didn't believe her at first, but then it all came tumbling down eventually. I guess Brock thought he could play us both. Keep us both dangling."

"I'm glad you both survived Brock's manipulation," Ian said. "Really, family is more important than anything else."

Brandy nodded and puffed out a breath. "Yeah, despite all the drama, and despite my mother constantly meddling, family is really who you can depend on."

Ian swallowed against the roughness of his throat. "Agreed. Take it from me, you don't want to put other agendas above your own family. If I could go back and change things with my dad, I would in a heartbeat. Even if it meant not starting up the company with Pete or ever meeting Ella."

Her brows lifted. "You have that many regrets?"

Ian rubbed the back of his neck. "My dad was a carpenter, you see, and wanted me to go into business with him. I used to work in his shop after school, and well, I told him I hated it."

"But . . . you didn't?"

Ian moved his hand over his jaw and released a sigh. "I mean, I hated to be kept so busy, away from friends—you know, teenager stuff. But building furniture has become my solace now. I wish I could tell my dad and thank him."

"Maybe he knows."

"What do you mean?"

Brandy lifted a shoulder. "My dad died, too, and sometimes I wonder if he's watching over my family. And maybe helps with the important stuff. Everly should really hate me, and I should hate her, because of Brock. But somehow, we're able to see past the crazy situation and trust each other. So maybe your dad knows about your workshop? It's kind of a tribute to him."

Ian couldn't speak for a moment. He wasn't a religious guy, and he didn't feel like Brandy was preaching any sort of doctrine. It was more like her personal observations and feelings. But he liked how the idea made the guilt ease. "I can only hope so," he said. "Living with regret about my dad has been rough."

"I don't even know your dad, but I'll bet he was proud

of you—no matter what you did. From the sound of it, your company was hugely successful, and you made a valiant effort at marriage."

Ian scoffed. Not because he didn't believe Brandy, but because she was pointing out the positives in everything. He'd been focusing on the negatives. "You should be a motivational speaker."

Her dimple appeared. "I don't think my philosophies would hold in front of the masses. I'm just a geeky accountant."

"You're an accountant?"

"Don't be so surprised. Blondes have brains."

Ian frowned. "I didn't mean anything like that—it's just that we might have something in common after all."

"What? Besides our tragic tales of betrayal?"

"I was a finance major in college."

Brandy laughed. "Ah. We can be geeks together—geeky neighbors, that is."

Duke barked, probably because of Brandy's laugh, and he now thought it was playtime.

"Deal." Ian extended his hand and she shook it. Her fingers were smooth and warm, and she let go much too quickly. But he wasn't going to dwell on how it felt to touch Brandy, or to have her in his home, or to have their heart-to-heart talk. No, he needed to make a decision, and soon.

"So do you work for a firm?" he asked.

"Freelance, actually." Brandy tucked some hair behind her ears. "I'm also the CFO for a nonprofit, Water for Kids. We build wells in Africa. Don't worry, Brock isn't on the board of directors."

"I'm impressed," Ian said. In fact, everything about Brandy was impressive.

Ten

BRANDY KNEW SHE SHOULD LEAVE Ian to his thoughts and decisions, but she felt reluctant to leave his cabin. She was surprised at how open he'd been about his failed marriage and his dad, and in turn, how she'd told him about the Brock situation. Well, everyone in Everly Falls knew about it, so it wasn't that big of a deal. Yet . . . talking to Ian tonight had been healing for her on a new level.

She realized that everyone, every place in the world, was dealing with heartbreak. And everyone was working through it in the way they knew best. Ian had sold his company in response to his divorce. But he'd also started a new business to honor the memory of his dad.

And Brandy was . . . well, she didn't know yet how deep she'd get into this new lifestyle of hers. Was it temporary, or would she stay here for months? So far, it had been fine, although completely different. She definitely hadn't expected to form a friendship with her standoffish neighbor. He wasn't standoffish at all. Just fiercely private.

"You can keep the rest of the brownies," Brandy said, rising from her chair.

Duke immediately rose, too, and wagged his tail. She scratched his head. "See you later, buddy."

"I'll walk you back." Ian pushed back in his chair.

"You don't have to." Brandy was pretty sure her protest was futile.

Yep.

Ian was already leading the dog to the front door and grabbing a jacket hanging on a nearby peg. His green eyes cut to her. "You didn't bring a jacket?"

"It wasn't cold when I left."

Instead of slipping on the jacket, he handed it to her.

"It's a short walk," she protested.

But Ian didn't drop his hand, so Brandy sighed and slipped it on. But she smiled at him. When he smiled back, the butterflies in her stomach leapt to life. Ian Hudson really was a handsome man, a courteous man, and someday a woman would snag him and treat him right. He deserved something good in his life.

Brandy walked past him out onto the porch, then headed down the stairs. Instead of following her like some bodyguard, Ian walked next to her, Duke running up ahead.

The stars had come out, and a soft wind stirred the trees above. The night was velvety black, but the path through the trees was well-defined enough to see with only a sliver of moonlight.

"I hope your mom's not upset with me," Ian said. "Since I have no intention of encouraging you to move back to Everly Falls."

Brandy looked over at him. "I'm that great of a neighbor?"

His gaze was steady on hers. "I think space from Brock and his manipulation will be good. I've listened to several relationship podcasts and read more than one self-help book on narcissists and their partners—you'll heal faster if he's completely out of your life."

"Ah, good point. I need to borrow that book—do you still have it?" Brandy stopped when they'd reached the clearing in front of her cottage.

"Somewhere, and you can borrow it."

Brandy nodded, looking up at him. "Thanks for listening to my tale of woe, and I hope everything goes okay if you do go to the funeral."

Ian's brow creased. "Yeah, me too." He scrubbed a hand through his hair. "Maybe we should exchange numbers. You know, in case I do leave. I can give you a heads-up."

"What about Duke? Want me to watch him?"

"Nah. I'll take him with me."

"All right." Brandy pulled out her phone, and Ian typed his number into it. Then she called it so he'd have her contact as well. "Good luck."

"Thanks." Ian retrieved his phone and created her contact. Then he shoved his hands into his pockets. "Good night, Brandy."

"Good night, Ian." She gave the dog a final scratch. "Bye, Duke."

Then, without thinking about what she was doing, she stepped forward and hugged Ian. It probably caught him off guard, but she felt like the man needed a hug. It took him a couple of seconds to wrap his arms around her and pull her close. Yep. There was that clean-showered man smell. She wasn't sure if the thudding of his heart was from the walk or from the hug. But she drew away before she could analyze it too much.

"See you later." She lifted a hand in a wave.

Ian said nothing, but she felt his gaze on her as she walked the rest of the way to the cottage. Her heart was pounding so hard that it pulsed in her ears. She hoped Ian knew that hug was innocent, friendly . . . from one neighbor to another who was going through a rough time.

After she went inside and closed the door, she moved to the front window to peer out. Ian had left with his dog.

"Well, then . . ." she whispered to herself. "Ian Hudson is a man of many layers. Not at all what I expected." She locked the door, then went through her bedtime routine while wondering if Ian had texted his ex-best-friend Pete, and what he'd decided to do.

After climbing into bed, she scanned her phone log. Her mother had called to update her on some town gossip. Everly had invited her to join her and Austin for a movie night in a few days. The friend group was currently active, with Steph telling everyone about her date from the night before, and how he might be "the one."

Seemed like Steph had already forgotten all about Ian. For that, Brandy was suddenly grateful. She kind of wanted him all to herself. Not romantically, of course—it wasn't like she was crushing on the man. She could just respect him and want the best for her new friend.

She made a couple of comments on the group text, then switched over to her emails. Nothing had come through from any clients that was urgent, so she'd reply to everything tomorrow. Next, she reached for the novel on her bedside table. She began to read, but realized after a couple of pages, she hadn't comprehended anything. Her mind was still on Ian—had he texted Pete by now?

Would it be too nosy to ask him? She had his number, so maybe she could casually ask if there was anything he needed her to check on at the cabin while he gone. Then he'd update her?

No . . . she'd let him be.

When she next opened her eyes, her bedroom lamp was still on, but sunlight streamed through her partly-opened bedroom curtains. She grabbed her phone to check the time—it was after eight in the morning.

"Oh no," she muttered. She'd overslept, and she had a full work day, which meant she'd be working until six or seven tonight.

Brandy scrambled out of bed and headed to the bathroom. She showered in record time, then cracked open the window to let out the steam. A banging sound came from the direction of Ian's cabin. What was he doing? Hammering on the roof?

The sound stopped, then other thudding sounds started up.

Brandy shouldn't worry about it—it was probably something with his furniture building. But still, she dressed and headed out of the cottage. She walked along the shortcut path until she could see through the trees enough to spot Ian loading something in the bed of his truck. He was barely balancing a bookcase.

"I can help," Brandy said, rushing out of the trees.

Ian startled and nearly dropped the bookcase. He caught it just before it landed in the dirt.

"Sorry," she breathed. "I didn't mean to scare you."

Ian's face twisted into a grimace as he lifted the bookcase again, and Brandy bent her knees to get her shoulder under the other side. Together, they got the bookcase into the bed of the truck.

"Thanks," he said, his voice gruff, his breath coming fast.

"Is there anything more?" Brandy eyed the other pieces in the back of the truck, neatly lined up against each other.

"That was the last piece." Ian brushed off his hands.

"Are you okay?" She turned her gaze on him to see a pretty good scrape on his arm. It wasn't bleeding much, but it probably stung. "Was that because of me?"

He lifted his arm and turned it. "No, that was from the door frame of the workshop. It's fine. Not my first run-in with a door."

His eyes were a somber green, darker than the leaves around them. He made a perusal of her, and Brandy suddenly realized that she must look a sight.

"Did you just get out of the shower or something?" he asked.

Brandy looked down at herself. Yeah . . . so she was barefoot and wore shorts and a T-shirt with no bra. *Welp.* She tugged the edge of her T-shirt, stretching it out a bit. "I heard the banging, and I thought . . ." What *had* she thought?

Ian's green eyes were now amused. "I was wrestling a bear or something?"

"No," Brandy said quickly. "I thought maybe you were mad about something and were, you know, throwing stuff."

His brows tugged together. "I don't throw stuff when I'm mad. I'm more the strong, silent type."

He was teasing, she knew. A laugh escaped her, then he smiled.

"Well, sorry all the same about startling you. Do you have first aid ointment for that scrape? I can get some if you don't."

He looked at his arm again. "It's fine. A little water goes a long way."

Okay, then. She looked at the truck bed. "Making your delivery?" *Yep. Stating the obvious.*

"Yeah."

Then she noticed the duffle bag on the porch. Had he

decided . . . ?"

"And I'm going to the funeral." The skin about his eyes had tightened. "I hope it's not a mistake, and it will bring closure, like you said. But there's been a wrinkle."

"Like what?" Brandy leaned against the side of the truck and folded her arms.

"Uh." He scrubbed a hand through his hair. "Ella called me after I texted Pete that I was coming. It's been a long time since I've heard her voice."

"Was that weird?"

"Yeah, but that's not the issue. She said that she missed me and couldn't wait to see me."

Brandy blinked. "Whoa."

"Yeah." Ian blew out a breath. "She kind of terrifies me."

It might have been funny coming at any other time, since Ian was a tall, imposing man, but Brandy understood. "So you wouldn't consider reconciliation with her?"

"Hell, no. Although, I might have to reread that self-help book to remind myself why it's a good thing to steer clear of her."

"Maybe download the audio and listen on your drive?"

The edge of his mouth lifted. "Nice idea."

"I think you need a plan."

"Plan for what?"

"You know, how long you'll stay at the funeral. What information you'll give out. Who you're willing to talk to. What time you'll leave to come back home. All of that."

Ian nodded at this. "Then I'm not second-guessing my decisions or letting her talk me into staying longer or talking more."

"Exactly."

"Or . . . I have another idea."

"What's that?"

Ian's gaze locked with hers. "What if *you* come with me? To be my moral support, or maybe more accurately, my babysitter. I know it's a big ask..."

His voice trailed off, probably because he noticed the shock on Brandy's face. He was asking her to go with him to his ex-mother-in-law's funeral?

"Never mind," he said. "My brain isn't working right. It's a work day for you, and—"

"I'll come," Brandy blurted out before she could consider all of the logistics. Her face and neck warmed, but she knew it was a good decision. All decisions that helped out a friend in need were good, right? "I mean, I can work on my laptop while you're driving. But I'm not coming as a babysitter, I'm coming as a friend."

Ian stared at her for a moment, like he couldn't believe she'd agreed. "Really? You'll come?"

She smiled because it looked like he was about to kneel before her and kiss her hand. "Really. I'll go pack a bag, then I'll be ready. Oh, and I'll get dressed, too."

Ian didn't smile at her quip. He looked more serious than ever. "Brandy, you don't have to come. I was just spitting out words. I don't think I slept last night."

It only took her a half second to reply. "All the more reason for you to have someone with you." She stepped toward him and rested her hand on his arm. "I can help drive, too. None of my work is urgent this week. I can catch up over the weekend when we're back."

He opened his mouth, then closed it. With a nod, he said, "Okay, but I owe you . . . something. I'll pay for everything, of course."

"Of course." Brandy flashed him a smile. "Give me about fifteen minutes?"

Eleven

IAN COULDN'T BELIEVE BRANDY HAD agreed to come with him to the funeral. He also couldn't believe that he'd *asked* her to come. But now that they were on their way, he was more than glad, and relieved.

His thoughts and emotions were a jumble. Sure, he was sad about Valerie and regretted losing touch with her. But Ella's voice last night had rocked him straight into his past—when he'd been in a dark place for a long time.

It wasn't until he'd broken all ties and had spent a few months living in his cabin that he'd finally been able to lift his head above water. But now, driving to the funeral home where he knew he'd come face-to-face with both Ella and Pete made him feel like he was standing at the edge of a diving board, and the water below had two circling sharks.

Duke napped on the bench behind them, and Brandy's fingers flew over her laptop keyboard as she typed. She'd explained her freelance work to him, and he was impressed that she managed a large stable of clients. She was planning on hiring an assistant in a few months to help her through April's tax season, although most of her clients filed quarterly taxes.

Ian's gaze strayed over to Brandy again. She'd been ready when he pulled his truck up to her cottage. Dressed and packed. Although he hadn't minded her just-showered look, he needed to keep his thoughts free of how beautiful she was, and how much he liked her dressed down, and how that hug last night had stirred new thoughts inside of him. Which only told him that his head was still a mess—she'd hugged him to be a friend, to offer comfort.

Yet thoughts of her body pressed against his were still fresh in his mind. Especially with her sitting only a couple of feet from him. He redirected his thoughts to the next batch of furniture orders awaiting him. The wood was on order, and he'd pick that up on his way back tomorrow. He didn't think Brandy would mind the short detour. As it was, they were nearly to the shipping company that would be their first stop of the morning.

Brandy stopped typing and looked up from her laptop. "Are we almost there?"

"Yeah, just up ahead," Ian said as he slowed the truck to take the final turn.

"Wow, that went fast." She closed her laptop, then stretched her arms in front of her. "I guess without Wi-Fi to distract me, I get through accounts a lot faster. I'm nearly halfway done with my day's work."

"You were typing like your fingers were on fire."

Brandy laughed. "There's that, too, and . . ." She bent to pull out her phone from her bag that sat on the floor of the truck. "My phone on silent helped, too." She began to scroll through whatever was on her phone.

Ian's mind flashed to Ella on her phone when he drove. She hated long car rides, but she seemed to entertain herself by texting—friends, she'd said. Now he wondered if Ella had been texting Pete that whole time. Whenever he'd asked who she was messaging, she never gave him any information.

"Oh wow, my mom texted me three times and called twice," Brandy said. "I told Everly I was going to a funeral with you, and I guess my sister told my mom."

Ian turned into the parking lot of the shipping center and drove up to the loading dock. When he put the truck into park, Brandy showed him her phone.

Sure enough, he could see the number of missed calls from "Mom."

"Do you mind if I call my mom? Or she'll just keep panicking. Then I can help you unload."

Ian was surprised she'd even asked. "I don't expect you to unload furniture. A couple of guys from the shipping company will do it."

"Okay." Brandy called her mother, and as Ian climbed out of the truck, he heard her say, "Hi, Mom. Before you ask a million questions, I'm fine."

He smiled to himself as he wondered how Brandy would handle her mother's interrogation. Lydia Kane was certainly a hands-on mother.

It didn't take long to get the furniture unloaded and tagged so it would be shipped to the right locations. When Ian climbed back in, Brandy smiled over at him.

"Good conversation?"

"She's full of questions about you, of course," Brandy said. "I couldn't answer most of them, so be prepared for an interrogation."

Ian smiled. "Uh, okay?"

She smirked and reached for the visor and flipped it down. "I'm kidding. I'm not going to interrogate you, and even if I did, I'm not going to tell my mom all about the mysterious man I'm with."

"Mysterious, huh?"

Brandy grabbed some sort of lip gloss out of her bag, then applied it while looking in the visor mirror. "Well, that's my mom's word." She flipped the visor up and looked over at him.

Now, her lips were glossy, and he swore he could smell strawberries. "Is she all right with you coming with me? I mean, she's kind of intense."

Brandy looked up at the ceiling. "I think it's more that she's protective." Her gaze shifted to his. "Or maybe she's trying to be more involved and in tune with my life. I lived away from Everly Falls during college and she never knew about all the guys I dated. I could have gone on dozens of road trips to funerals, for all she knew."

Ian frowned as he pulled out of the parking lot. "Wait. How many guys are we talking here?"

"I just dated casually. Brock was my first official boyfriend. What about you? How much did you date before you met Ella?"

Ian could feel Brandy's interested gaze on him as he turned onto the main road. "Is this part of your interrogation?" He glanced over at her, and she mimicked zipping her lips closed.

He chuckled.

"Let's make a deal," she said in a slow tone. "What's said in this truck doesn't go anywhere else."

"Not even to your sister?"

Brandy gasped. "I don't tell my sister everything, you know."

Ian smirked. "All right, fair enough."

"So . . . how many girlfriends have you had?"

"One besides Ella." Ian slowed at a traffic light. "In high school, although we both knew things wouldn't progress past that. In college, I dated some, but never any type of serious relationship. I was too into my classes and planning out my company with Pete."

Brandy nodded, then she pointed to a café up ahead. "Do you mind stopping for something to eat? I didn't have time for breakfast since I slept in this morning."

"Sure." Ian pulled the truck into the parking lot. "Duke probably needs to get out for a second, and I wouldn't want your mother to think I've starved you."

"Funny," Brandy said. "I can just run in really quick. Do you want anything?"

"Maybe some coffee."

She paused before opening the door. "I can take a turn driving when I get back. I don't mind."

Ian appreciated the offer, he really did. In his marriage to Ella, he'd done all the driving. "I'll let you know if I get too tired."

Brandy climbed out of the truck, and he watched her walk into the café. Then he climbed out, too, and opened the door for Duke. As he waited for Brandy, he checked his phone. Ella had texted him twice. Once telling him to drive safe. Then again, saying she was so grateful he was coming. Her language was gushing, and it made a pit harden in Ian's stomach. He couldn't remember the last time she'd been so enthusiastic about his presence. Well, he could—early into their relationship and marriage.

By the time Brandy came out of the café, with two cups of something steaming and a pastry sack, he was wondering if he'd made a mistake in all of this. He could text Ella and Pete that he wasn't able to make the funeral after all. He loaded Duke into the truck, then climbed in the driver's seat and started the engine.

Brandy seemed to notice his mood shift. "Is everything all right?"

Ian turned out of the parking lot. "Wondering if I'm

making the right decision. I just read my texts—several are from Ella."

"Oh?" Brandy handed him one of the coffee cups. "Is she love-bombing you again?"

He might have laughed if it weren't so very accurate.

Brandy's eyes widened. "She is?"

"Judge for yourself." Ian handed over his phone, then turned the corner onto the main road.

"Just flew in from San Jose. I hope you drive safe, honey," Brandy read, then paused. "Is that her endearment for you or is she from Texas?"

"She's a sweet talker when she wants something."

Brandy read the next one. "I can't wait to see you. Thank you so much for coming. You've always been such a rock in my life." She set the phone on the console between them. "Ew."

"Yeah, ew."

"Ian, I hate to say this, but I think your ex-wife might want you back."

He shook his head, not wanting to believe it. Also not wanting to deal with it. He was feeling triggered by Ella's words, so he just had to remember the self-help books he'd read and recognize her sugary manipulation. He wouldn't make the same mistake twice. But that didn't mean her words didn't have an effect on his emotions.

"She doesn't want me back," he said. "She's probably feeling nostalgic going through her mom's things." He sighed. "I'm so glad you're coming with me, Brandy. I'd be heading back home if you weren't."

"Does she know I'm coming?"

"Not yet." He sipped from the coffee, hoping the caffeine would clear his muddled thoughts. Truth was, his stomach was in knots, and he couldn't manage more than a few sips. "She'll probably think we're dating or something."

"Well, you can set her straight."

"What if . . ." Ian glanced over at Brandy. "What if we pretended we're in a relationship. You know, just for the time we're around Ella. She might back off, and then after the funeral, I'll never have to see her again. Case closed."

Brandy didn't answer at first, and Ian couldn't decipher her expression. The next road turned onto the highway, and the truck tires hummed, creating more white noise.

"Or maybe that's a lousy idea," he added. "Ella can draw her own conclusions, and we just won't correct her. Or we can just say we're neighbors, like we are, and—"

"I'll do it," Brandy said suddenly. "Me showing up with you will make her suspicious anyway, and I'll never see her again after the funeral. It's not like she knows anything about me. Should I use a fake name? That would be kind of fun."

Ian smiled. "Whatever you want . . . although I don't trust myself to not slip up."

"All right, I'll just be Brandy. Mysterious Brandy."

"I like it."

She laughed. "My sister used to make up boyfriends to deal with certain situations—it was kind of hilarious. I thought she was nuts, but now I understand."

"Thanks, Brandy, really." Ian reached for her hand and squeezed. "I mean it. You're bailing me out, so I'm pretty much at your mercy and in your debt."

She squeezed his hand in return, then released him. "I think it's good for me to get out of the problems in my own head for a while."

"So you'll just live inside my problems instead?"

"Yep. I feel like I have a partner in crime or something."

Ian smirked. "You know, Ella is a smart woman, so we'll have to be smarter."

"How do we do that?"

"We might have to resort to PDA. To be convincing that we're in a relationship."

"Ah." Brandy tucked some escaped hair behind her ears. "I think I can handle that, Mr. Hudson."

His heart began a slow pound. Holding hands with Brandy, or even kissing her, brought on a whole other set of emotions.

Twelve

BRANDY HATED TO WAKE IAN, but according to the GPS on her phone, the next turn-off would take them to the funeral home. He'd booked a nearby hotel so they could get ready there, then head to the funeral. The sun was high overhead, and Brandy suspected Ian hadn't slept at all the night before, since he'd been sleeping now for three hours.

But as she turned off the highway and slowed at the first traffic light, he opened his eyes. For a second, he didn't move. Then he snapped his head to look at her. "We're here?"

"We're here."

He groaned and rubbed a hand over his face. "Sorry, I didn't mean to sleep so long. You should have awakened me."

"No, I shouldn't have," Brandy countered in a light tone. "You needed the sleep. We have a covert mission to undertake, and I need you at the top of your game."

Ian gave her a small smile. The light turned green, and she pressed on the gas pedal.

"Thank you, Brandy, even though you disobeyed my

wishes," he teased.

"Ha. In this case, I was happy to ignore you."

Ian stifled a yawn. "I can't believe I slept so long." His gaze moved to her again. "Are you okay? Tired? Hungry?"

She cast him a smile. "I'm fine. The drive was beautiful, and Duke shared some doggy stories with me."

"Good job, Duke." He reached back and scratched the dog's head. Then he turned his gaze to the passing buildings and shops. "We can grab something to eat before the funeral. The viewing is for an hour, so we don't have to be there right at the beginning."

"All right, what sounds good?"

"You choose," Ian said. "I could eat anything."

She cast him a glance. "All right . . ." The hotel came into view, and across the street was a diner. "We could eat at that diner. Keep things simple."

"Sounds good to me."

Brandy parked the truck, and they climbed out. Ian insisted on carrying her bag, and she held on to the leash with Duke. As they walked into the lobby of the hotel, Brandy marveled that she was suddenly in San Diego with her new neighbor and his dog. Attending a funeral, of all things.

It didn't take long for Ian to check in, and they walked along the corridor leading to the rooms. "We're on the ground floor because they don't want pets in the elevator. Our rooms are across from each other." He handed over her room key.

"Okay, no problem." Brandy scanned the hallway of doors and had a sudden thought. "What if Ella and Pete are at the same hotel?"

Ian's brows shot up. "Not to worry. They'll stay at a five-star somewhere. I purposely reserved something a little more basic."

"That makes sense."

"How long do you need to get ready?" he asked, and she heard the trepidation in his voice.

"Maybe an hour?"

At the look on his face, she laughed. "Kidding. Give me fifteen minutes. I need to get ready to play my part."

Relief crossed Ian's face as they reached their doors.

"Sorry, I don't mean to tease you," she said. "I know this is stressful all the way around."

"You can give me crap all you want," he said, but his tone was somber. "I don't think I'd be here if you weren't. So thank you again."

"You're welcome, Ian, truly. But you don't need to thank me every hour."

His smile appeared, which made her heart warm. "Okay. I'll cut back on that if you insist."

She moved her bag to her hotel room door, then scanned the key card. Ian headed into his room with Duke, and Brandy walked into her own room. The place was pretty basic, but she didn't mind. Brock always insisted on the best of the best, and it sounded like Ian's ex-wife was of a similar nature. And while Brandy could see that Ian's cabin was extremely nice, and he probably had a nest egg with the selling of a successful company, he was down-to-earth, and not pretentious in the way Brock could be.

Brandy set her bag on the bed and unzipped it. Pulling out the dress she'd brought, she decided she'd need to iron it after all. She set up the ironing board and plugged in the iron, then headed into the bathroom. Her ponytail was falling out, and she tugged out her ponytail holder, then ran a brush through her hair. Turning on the sink, she ran some water through her hair to tamp down the flyaways and the artificial wave from the ponytail.

Next, she plugged in her straightening iron. Her hair had no natural wave or curl to it, unlike Everly, but ponytails or messy buns made it kink weird.

As she applied makeup, she wondered what Ella looked like. What sort of woman had Ian Hudson fallen in love with and married? Not that his type should concern her. Yeah, she was going to be his fake girlfriend for a short time, but beyond that, she was enjoying a friendship with a man that didn't involve the potential of dating. It was kind of refreshing, really. Because she needed to be *Brandy* for a while. Not another man's girlfriend, trying to measure up to whatever his ideal was.

Which of course was the very definition of being in a relationship with a narcissist. She still wondered how she'd missed the signs. Probably because she'd really fallen in love with Brock—or at least she thought she had. Who knew anymore? Her brain was definitely a mess. Numbers were straightforward. Add them up, subtract them, multiply or divide them. They never lied. They couldn't. Two plus two would always equal four.

Thirty minutes later, Brandy headed out of her room. So . . . she hadn't been that quick. When she'd texted Ian she was running behind, he'd sent an eye-rolling emoji, which made her laugh. She hadn't thought of him as an emoji person, so it was kind of entertaining.

She found him in the lobby, waiting alone. Ian wore a suit that screamed expensive, and he was freshly shaven. "No Duke?"

He looked up and stilled, his gaze scanning her body. Slowly, he rose to his feet, his green eyes locked on her. Brandy's gaze was locked on him, too. Ian in a suit should come with a warning. *Watch out. Tall, dark, and handsome coming your way.* He said something about the dog, and Brandy had to force herself to pay attention to his words.

"I fed Duke already, and he'll be fine until we get back. Besides, I don't want him around Ella."

Brandy moved her gaze upward to focus on Ian's eyes and not the way his very expensive suit seemed tailored to him down to the last centimeter. "Why not?"

"She used the dog as one of her justifications for her affair, even though we'd only had Duke a few months, and her affair with Pete had been going on much longer." The words tumbled out as if Ian was trying not to feel the painful memory as he spoke.

"Then I agree," Brandy said. "Ella doesn't deserve to see Duke. He's too sweet of a boy to be exposed to such a vixen."

"Exactly." A smile lifted Ian's mouth. "So . . . I think we need to start acting our parts when we walk out of the hotel. You know, to be comfortable with it all."

"Of course." Her voice sounded small and her chest felt tight. And she was pretty sure a new horde of butterflies had joined the original horde in her stomach. "I'll follow your lead."

His mouth quirked, and his gaze moved over her again. If he kept this up, she'd be red as a radish by the time they reached the funeral home. Ian extended his hand, and it took Brandy a second to realize he wanted her to take it.

So she did.

Ian's fingers threaded through hers, and Brandy's entire body seemed to sigh. His hand was warm, and his skin was not soft, but not rough. More like the skin of a man who worked with his hands for a living.

She'd wondered about the scar across his knuckles, though. "What happened to your hand?"

He looked down at their linked fingers. "Slid into home

base in a high school game. The infield wasn't exactly power-dirt."

"Stitches?"

"Seventeen."

She nodded, and they walked out of the hotel, hand in hand, then crossed the street to the diner.

"Did I tell you that you look beautiful?" Ian asked, his green eyes once again on her.

"You didn't. Is that a fake girlfriend compliment or a real one?"

Ian's hold on her tightened. "Everything I say to you is real. Everything I say to Ella will be fake."

Brandy laughed. "All right, then. I'll play by the same rule. And by the way, I like your suit—you make a striking businessman."

His eyes filled with amusement. "Fake or real?"

"Real," she clarified.

"Are you a woman who likes men in suits, or more the worn jeans, flannel shirt type?"

Brandy bit her lip, pretending to consider. "I think a man—or at least the man of my dreams—will look great in both. Equally."

"You have a dream man?"

"Uh, that just slipped out. No comment."

Ian opened the door of the diner, and released her hand so she could walk in ahead of him.

What's next? Brandy wondered. More hand-holding? Sitting close together in a booth with his arm around her? A light kiss? Her pulse thrummed as Ian spoke to the hostess about a table for two.

Table for two . . .

A server with turquoise glasses and a pixie haircut embellished with blue streaks led them to a booth of brown pleather.

Ian nudged Brandy's shoulder and said in a quiet voice, "I want details."

She pressed her lips together and shook her head.

He chuckled, then draped his arm over her shoulder and pulled her into a side hug.

"Is this all right?" the server asked, her eyes huge behind her glasses.

"It's great, thanks," Ian answered, because Brandy was trying to find her voice.

This PDA with Ian was . . . kind of thrilling. And it shouldn't be. It was all fake anyway, so her pulse needed to calm down.

She slid into the booth on one side, and instead of Ian sitting on the other side, he slid in after her, so they were right next to each other. Unless Brandy kept moving around the booth. But Ian had grasped her hand again, so apparently, they were going to sit shoulder to shoulder.

"Here are the menus," the server continued. Her red name tag said *Shaela*. "Can I get you drinks to start?"

"Water's fine," Brandy said.

"Water for me, too," Ian added.

After the server walked away, Brandy said, "I think you're liking this PDA thing too much. I mean, Ella's nowhere in sight." Not that she'd recognize her if she was.

Ian looked down at their linked hands and rubbed a thumb over her knuckles. "Like I said, we need to practice, so it will all look natural later on."

Brandy couldn't stop her scoff.

"What? You think I'm crushing on you?"

She tamped down a blush. "Maybe? I can't read your mind, but we don't have to sit all cozy in a booth like teenagers."

Ian grinned.

Brandy laughed.

"Okay, how about this?" He scooted away from her maybe two inches.

"*So* much better," Brandy teased.

He released her hand and picked up the menu. With his eyes on the food choices, he said, "When you miss holding my hand, I'm all yours."

Brandy sighed dramatically. "Fine." She grabbed his hand and tugged it onto her lap.

Ian chuckled. "I knew you weren't really complaining."

She had no idea what was real or what was fake anymore, but they held hands until their food came. And only then did she release Ian's hand to eat.

Thirteen

WAS IAN CRUSHING ON BRANDY? Maybe a little, but that's all he could allow his mind to process. She was beautiful—gorgeous, actually—and he liked talking to her. Being with her was . . . fun. Something he'd never had with Ella. Their relationship had been so intense at first, and he'd walked on eggshells around her emotions, hoping she'd approve of him. Of course, it took her affair for him to realize how ridiculous he'd been. How self-deprecating, how insecure, how codependent.

But Brandy . . . maybe they were connecting so quickly because of their shared issues with previous relationships? What was that called? Trauma bonding? If that was the case, was it good or bad? Would the proverbial rose-colored glasses crack after this road trip and leave them both worse off than they'd started?

Whatever it was, Ian didn't know if he could trust his judgment right now. Their meal was almost finished, and then there would be no more delays. He would be facing his past, literally in the face. One part of him wanted to be back at his cabin, more specifically in his workshop. Measuring wood. Cutting it to specification. Fitting pieces together. Sanding. Staining. Working on projects he could start while knowing the exact outcome. No surprises. No ups and downs. No crushing disappointments or betrayals.

"Would you like dessert?" Shaela, the server, had returned.

"I'm fine," Ian said, then looked at Brandy.

"I'm fine, too. Thanks, though."

Another memory raked through Ian about Ella. Whenever they'd gone out to eat, she'd been snippety with the servers. Ella's complaints over the food or service were always vocal, so the restaurant managers frequently comped her meals. Now, he could see it for what it was—a power trip for Ella.

Ian picked up the bill, and they walked to the register to pay, Brandy's hand in his. This made him smile. If anyone was going to be his fake girlfriend for a couple of days, she was perfect for that job.

He paid at the register, then they headed outside. Since the funeral home was only a block away, Ian said, "You okay to walk in those shoes?" Brandy's heels definitely made her taller next to him, but he'd still have to bend down to kiss her.

All right, his thoughts were way out there, and he needed to rein them in.

"Sure," Brandy said. "I think it would be easier to walk than to try to climb into your truck in this dress."

Yeah, her black dress was plain, but it followed her curves, which made the dress not plain at all. He wasn't complaining, of course. She wore small pearl earrings and her pearl necklace. Simple and elegant. She'd certainly contrast Ella, if Ian were to guess.

"Okay, but if your feet hurt, I can come back for the truck and drive you to the hotel."

"I'm sure I'll be fine, but thanks for the offer."

He nodded, and they set out in the late afternoon. They were close enough to the ocean that he could smell the tang of salt in the air mixed with whatever perfume Brandy was wearing—a subtle, light floral scent.

Their hands stayed linked, and it was a good thing because just as they crossed into the parking lot of the funeral home, Ella and Pete stepped out of the building. Pete pulled out a cigarette and lit it. Ian had forgotten he smoked. After taking the first drag, he handed it over to Ella, who put it in her mouth.

Ian was so shocked, he might have stumbled if he weren't gripping Brandy's hand. Ella had sworn off smoking because her dad had died of lung cancer. There was no way she could be a smoker—at least while they were married—was there? What else didn't he know?

"Is that . . . them?" Brandy whispered.

The pair hadn't seen them yet, and Ian whispered back, "Yep."

She squeezed his hand, which was reassuring, but his stomach had turned to stone. In the next moment, they'd be spotted.

"Ian!" Ella saw him first as she turned her head. Her smile went wide. Yep, she was dolled up as usual. Deep-red lipstick, thick eyeliner, false eyelashes. Diamonds at her ears, throat, and wrists. Her black dress was low cut, and she wore heels a mile high. Ella had trimmed her hair short. It was usually about shoulder length, but now her hair was cropped below her ears in a severe A-line. Her dark brows matched her equally dark hair, which he knew she dyed religiously since her true color was a faded brown.

Ella's smile slipped when she spotted Brandy. "Who's this?" she said, without wasting another moment on any sort of welcome.

"This is Brandy." Ian knew his grasp on her hand had become a death grip. His gaze shifted to Pete, who blew out a plume of smoke. The guy was as blond as ever, but he'd lost the devil-may-care gleam that had always been in his eyes. New lines creased his face, and his usually robin-blue eyes were a cement gray. Pete was also a guy who worshiped at the gym, but he looked like he'd lost a lot of weight—and it wasn't good weight to lose.

"Hi there, Ian." Pete nodded to Brandy as he shifted on his feet. Was he nervous? Feeling awkward? "Nice to meet you, Brandy. Where're you from?"

Before she could answer, Ian cut in. "Brandy, this is Ella and Pete."

"Nice to meet you," Brandy said in a perfectly even, pleasant voice. "So very sorry for your loss."

"Thank you," Ella murmured, but her eyes narrowed as her gaze raked over Brandy. "I didn't know you were bringing someone," she said to Ian, setting her hand on her hip. The diamonds on her fingers caught the afternoon light. He didn't look long enough to see if one might be an engagement or wedding ring. As it was, Ella's nut-brown eyes were full of questions and suspicion.

"It was last minute," Ian said. "Brandy didn't know she could come until this morning." A small white lie, but the sooner they moved past this initial meeting, the better.

"I'm so glad I could clear my schedule." Brandy looped her other hand around his arm, leaning into him.

"Well." Ella looked over at Pete. "Take them inside and show them where to sit. You'll have to bring out an extra chair for . . . Brandy." Her nose wrinkled. "I'll be in soon."

Would it all be this easy? Ian followed Pete inside. Mournful organ music came from the chapel room, playing a quiet melody. They walked through a foyer that contained a couple of tables filled with framed pictures of Valerie. Ian stopped by the registry and signed his name, then handed the pen to Brandy.

She took the pen with a quick glance at him, then wrote her own name on the line below his.

"This way," Pete said. "Ella's got you in the front row with us." He gave a pointed look to Brandy, which she returned with a guileless smile.

Good for her. Ian could have kissed her then and there.

Beyond the next doorway, the chapel area was about half-filled with people waiting for the service to begin. A couple of others milled about the tables with the pictures on it, and likely the family members were in the room with the casket.

"We'll sit in the back, thanks." Ian draped an arm about Brandy's shoulder and steered her toward one of the tables.

Pete was probably shocked, but Ian didn't care. He was here for Valerie, not for Ella or Pete. They didn't all need to sit together, and with the divorce, he didn't need to sit in the family row.

"Is he still staring?" Ian whispered to Brandy.

"No, he's gone into the other room."

He blew out a breath, keeping his arm around her as they walked to a table of photos. "We made it through the initial greeting. Now only three more hours to go."

The photos were of Valerie's younger years—a time before Ian knew her. She was posed at a beach, in a park, at a Fourth of July celebration.

Brandy moved her arm around his waist so she was nestled right next to him. "How are you holding up?"

"I don't know yet," Ian said with a grimace. "Sorry if I crushed your hand out there."

She gave a soft laugh. "It's fine. I'm tougher than I look."

"Yeah . . . you've said that before."

"If Ella had a kitchen knife with her, I wouldn't have been surprised if she'd stabbed me with it."

"She's not happy you came," Ian mused. "I sort of liked seeing the surprise on her face. And the jealousy."

"It's weird that she'd be jealous since she divorced you, but I think you're right."

Ian absently stroked his fingers along her shoulder as they stood together. "It's all in the books I've been reading. Classic narcissist, really."

"I'm borrowing one when we get back to Everly Falls."

"Sure thing."

"Now, tell me about the good part of your marriage—your mother-in-law."

Ian led her to the next table, with photos of an older Valerie, as a mom and wife. "Ironic, isn't it? Most people complain about their mother-in-law, but not me. She was an amazing human. I remember her showing me some of these photos during visits." Some of the pictures showed Ella, too, and her dad. The smiling family made Ian realize just how much he'd missed out on as a kid. No mom around, and a dad who he'd been at odds with most of the time.

Valerie's hazel eyes smiled out from the photos of her. Her brown hair was almost always in its signature clip, holding back her naturally curly hair from her face. She had a kind smile and a loving nature. Ella took after her more stoic father, in both looks and personality.

"My favorite memory of Valerie is playing cards with her," Ian said in a slow tone. "We'd play late into the night, long after Ella would give up and go to bed. Those nights, we got into the best conversations. We talked about everything—science, art, crime, music. Valerie was well read and served on a bunch of charity boards. She talked me into donating to more than one."

He gave a soft laugh. "She could be very persuasive." Which was probably where Ella got it from, though Valerie used her persuasion for good causes. "But Valerie could also listen. When I talked to her, I knew she cared—I could feel it. She didn't miss a thing, and asked the most interesting questions. I don't remember the personality of my own mother, but suddenly I didn't care about what might have been missing from my childhood. Not when I was around Valerie. She brought something into my life that filled that hole."

He hadn't realized his voice had grown emotional, not until Brandy began to slowly run her hand along his back. "I'm really sorry you lost that, Ian," she said in a gentle tone. "But I'm also glad you were such good friends."

"Thanks," he whispered, then cleared his throat. "Anyway, like I said before, losing Valerie was the worst part of the divorce. And now . . . she's gone for good."

Brandy wrapped both of her arms about his waist in a side hug, and Ian bent to kiss the top of her head. It wasn't part of the act—the gesture had come naturally. He knew she wouldn't read into it more than what they'd agreed upon, but suddenly, he wished they weren't both pretending.

The door opened, and out of the corner of his eye, Ian could see it was Ella. He kept his arm around Brandy, hoping she would continue past them without a word. But that was too much to expect. She stopped on his other side.

"Remember this day?" she said, pointing to a picture.

The photo contained a smiling Valerie and Ella—her college graduation day. No, Ian hadn't been there, but Ella had told him about it.

"Your mom was so proud of you." Ian didn't want to reminisce with her. He wanted to stay in the warm cocoon he had with Brandy.

Ella turned a simpering gaze on him. "I remember the first time she told you about my graduation day. Wasn't that the first time you'd met her?"

"It was." Ian felt stiff. Uncomfortable.

Ella moved closer to the table and peered over at Brandy. "Are your parents still living, Brandy?"

Wasn't that a tacky question at a funeral?

Brandy dropped one of her arms from Ian, although she kept one arm about his waist. "My mom's still alive."

Ella's dark brows lifted. "So you lost your dad? How long ago?"

Ian felt the tension radiating through Brandy. "Maybe we should go see the casket before the service starts. It's almost time."

Ella pulled her daggered gaze from Brandy and gave him a sad smile. "Right. I'll come with you. I can't believe Mom is truly gone."

Ian was curious about when Valerie's cancer had come back, and if her passing was quick and merciful, but he didn't want to involve himself with Ella any more than he had to. Maybe he could ask Pete, but then again, Ian didn't want to talk to him either.

Brandy shifted, and he dropped his arm from about her shoulders. She reached for his hand, and they walked with Ella to the viewing room. Stepping inside, Ian could appreciate the reverence of seeing Valerie lying prone. It wasn't her, though—not the Valerie he knew. Only a shell of her body remained, and without her vibrant personality, the person in the casket seemed to be a wax creation at a museum.

Ella spoke to him again, but Ian wasn't listening. He kept his gaze on the casket and thanked Valerie in his mind. *Thank you for showing me what a good mother is like. Thank you for teaching me that family is important. Thank you for loving me no matter what else happened.*

Fourteen

Brandy hated Ella. Well, maybe that was too strong of a word. It was clear the woman had done a number on Ian, and even though Brandy didn't know how the next couple of hours would go, she was grateful she could be here to support him.

As they sat toward the back of the funeral service, Brandy was surprised to note that Pete and Ella didn't seem to be all that lovey-dovey. She'd expected the pair of them to act like they were the loves of each other's lives. After all, their affair had broken up a marriage. Maybe all wasn't well in dreamland?

Listening to the service was kind of interesting. Brandy had never attended a funeral of someone she hadn't known in real life. It was quickly clear, though, that Valerie was a woman she would have liked.

Next to her, Ian remained stoic. Emotionless, really, although she knew he was feeling something. His hand had a death grip on hers again. She placed her other hand atop his and slowly rubbed his fingers. His grip eased, and he threw her a small smile. That's when she saw that his eyes were red rimmed.

Brandy held back a sigh. She knew Ian had to go through this process, but she'd be happy when it was over for him, and he could release some of these heavy burdens he carried.

At the front of the room, Ella stood and walked to the podium. Her name was next on the program. She touched a tissue to her eyes, then looked out at the audience, a smile on her face. Although with her deep-red lipstick, it might have been mistaken for a grimace.

"Thank you all for coming," Ella said. "My mother always said that a party isn't a party without her loved ones present." Her voice broke, and Brandy felt a tiny seed of sympathy for the woman—she *had* lost her mother and she *was* grieving. So that made Ella somewhat human. As the woman continued speaking, Brandy's own thoughts turned to her father's funeral. It had been many years now, and her mother was doing great. But there was still a blank space in their lives. She remembered feeling sad that her father wouldn't be at her wedding to Brock.

Everly likely felt that sting now that she was engaged to Austin. Brandy was so happy for her sister to have found a man as devoted as Austin. He'd moved to Everly Falls for her sister, bringing his daughter along. That was devotion if she'd ever seen it.

Ella's speech seemed to be the longest of them all— which of course she had the prerogative to do. Brandy glanced over at Ian. He was staring straight ahead at nothing in particular. What was going through his mind? What kind of flips was his heart doing while listening to his ex-wife expound on memories of her mother?

"Are you okay?" she whispered.

He seemed to come out of his deep thoughts. "Yeah." But the skin about his eyes was tight.

Then . . . Ella said Ian's name. They both looked toward the front of the room.

"When Ian and I married, my mother said, 'Don't lose this man. He's the best thing that's happened to our family in a long time.'"

Ella was full-on crying now, and she wiped at more tears, sniffling. "Life is hard, for all of us, and we all have regrets. But losing a wonderful mother like Valerie has reminded me what to value in life. And I intend on reversing some of those regrets."

A shiver ran through Brandy at her words, because Ella was staring straight at Ian.

"Oh boy," he muttered to himself, but Brandy heard it.

Ella said a few other things, wiped her eyes some more, then concluded.

The next and final speaker was the reverend, but his words were like white noise in Brandy's mind. What had Ella meant by her words? And why had she been staring at Ian?

"Wanna get out of here?" he whispered.

"Aren't we going to the graveside part?"

"Yeah, but we can meet everyone there."

"Sure." Brandy rose to her feet, and she was pretty sure that several people noticed them leaving. She tried not to feel self-conscious about that. This was Ian's call.

Once they stepped outside, the air had cooled with the sun setting against the western horizon. Ian tugged off his tie and shoved it into his pocket. He wasn't touching her, holding her hand, or draping his arm over her shoulder. Apparently, they'd practiced their fake romance enough.

Brandy hurried alongside him, her heels clicking on the cement sidewalk on the way back to their hotel. Ian's face was set like stone, and he seemed to have forgotten all about her. It was fine—he needed to sort out his thoughts—but her feet were starting to hurt. Her shoes weren't built for practically running.

As they reached the corner to cross the street, Ian finally clued in to her presence. His gaze slid over her. "Sorry," he rasped. "I'm just . . ." He exhaled. "That was a lot."

"It's fine," she said. "Tell me what I can do to help."

His gaze again scanned her, and when his eyes lifted to meet hers, he said, "You're already doing it, Brandy. I know I need to go to the graveside service, but if I hear one more word from Ella . . . I'm going to lose it."

Brandy stepped forward. "Come on. Let's go see Duke for a bit, then we'll head to the cemetery in the truck. You don't even have to get out if you don't want. Or maybe we can go after the service, and you can pay your respects to Valerie's final resting place alone."

Ian seemed to think all this over. "Can we play it by ear? I just need some time to process all that's gone on."

"Yeah, of course."

He seemed relieved, and they crossed the street together. Inside the hotel, Brandy slipped off her heels.

Ian noticed. "Are your feet killing you?"

"They'll survive, but I'm going to put on my sandals, even though it will be less formal."

He nodded at this. As they walked down the hallway toward their rooms, Ian said, "I think I'm going to have to block her number. And it's time I talked to Pete. I know we were at a funeral, but he doesn't look happy at all. He's changed a lot."

"How so?"

"He looks ten years older," Ian said as they paused by their rooms. "I think Ella's done a number on him. The guy needs to bail to save himself. Even though he betrayed me, too, I know what it's like to be the target of Ella. I wouldn't wish that on my worst enemy—which he is."

"Maybe you can talk to him tonight after everything is done?" Brandy suggested. "You know, get it over with."

"Yeah, I think that's what I'll do."

Brandy nodded and turned to open her door, but Ian crossed the hallway and bent to kiss her cheek.

She froze, her pulse in overdrive.

"Thank you, Brandy," he said. "I know I keep saying that."

She stared after him as he slipped inside his hotel room. As she stood in the hallway for another minute, her mind raced. That kiss on the cheek hadn't felt fake, and neither had all the gratitude speeches. Finally, she opened her door and went inside her room. It had all been a lot. She agreed with Ian on that point.

She couldn't imagine being faced with Brock in this way, and they hadn't been married. But betrayal was betrayal, and that's why she didn't know if she could trust the emotions running through her right now. Protective toward Ian, angry toward Ella and Pete, who were strangers to her, disgust toward Brock—well, that wasn't anything new.

Brandy sat on the armchair in the corner of the room and scrolled through her phone. She'd had it on silent since the diner, and only now did she see the two missed calls and multiple texts from Everly.

Brandy frowned as she opened the string of texts, which she read backward.

Now I'm worried about you. Call me ASAP.

Mom wants to talk to you. I think the pain medicine they sent her home with has given her major anxiety—more than usual!

We're getting released soon, but we have an appointment with an orthopedic surgeon on Monday. I'll be staying with Mom.

They're sending the X-rays to a surgeon—she might need surgery.

They think Mom has an injured arm, but is otherwise ok.

Mom's fine, but she was in a car wreck. I'm on my way to the hospital now. Call me!

Brandy called her sister, and in two rings, Everly answered. "Everly! I just saw all your texts. How's Mom doing?"

"Are you all right? Where are you?"

"I'm fine." Brandy stood and began to pace the small hotel room. "Just got out of the funeral service. We're heading to the cemetery next. What happened with Mom? How did she wreck?"

"She was rear-ended pretty hard coming out of the grocery store," Everly said. "There's a police report that probably has more details, but I think Mom pulled out in front of someone."

"And she's going to need surgery for her arm?"

"I don't think so. The tech was talking about things I couldn't see on the X-ray. I was just texting as news came in." Everly sighed. "It's Mom's mental state that's worrying me. Her mind is frenzied, so I'm hoping that's just the pain medication, and it will wear off."

Brandy exhaled. "Wow, I'm sorry. I should come back tonight. I'll talk to Ian."

As if summoned by the mere mention of his name, someone knocked on the door. Brandy moved to look through the peephole, even though she knew it could only be one person. She opened the door and waved him in as Everly continued to talk.

"Mom's settled in the living room, ordering everyone around," Everly said. "I'm hiding out in the kitchen to take a break. Believe me, there's no rush for you to come back, but I'm sure by tomorrow I'll want a break."

"Are you sure you're okay?" Brandy asked her sister.

Ian gave her a questioning look. He leaned against the TV console and folded his arms, intent on what she was saying.

"I'm fine," Everly said. "Austin is here and Ruby from next door. Between the three of us, it's probably overkill. But Mom definitely wants to talk to you. She can't figure out why you're not here."

"OK, put her on the phone," Brandy said, meeting Ian's gaze. "Mom?"

"Brandy, I've been so worried about you," her mother said in a rush.

"I'm fine, Mom," she said. "You're the one who was in a car accident. How are you doing?"

"Oh, I hurt my arm." Mom laughed. "Can you believe it? First time in my life I've had an X-ray. I didn't even see that car coming. One minute the road was clear, and the next minute, *wham*. The X-ray tech was around your age and has such a nice job. I told Everly that's what she should do with her life instead of working at a craft store. Everly said you won't be back until tomorrow. Why are you going to be gone so long?"

The pain medication was definitely making her mom wig out. "I'll be home tomorrow, Mom. Look, I need to go. I'll call you a little later. Everly can keep me posted, too."

After hanging up with her mom, Brandy met Ian's concerned gaze.

"What's going on?" he asked.

She filled him in on the details that she knew so far about her mom's accident, then she said, "I can't believe that of all times, this happens when I'm out of town. I don't know if I should stay here overnight, but Everly said not to worry about coming home early."

"We could head back tonight," Ian said in a gentle tone. "I'd be fine driving."

Brandy bit her lip. She knew Ian would switch their plans, but her mom was in good hands. "Let me just call my sister again. Double check."

"Do you want me to wait in the hall?"

"No, it's fine." She gave him a brief smile. "I'm not going to tell her any secrets."

Ian nodded.

So Brandy called Everly and was reassured, once again, that everything was under control and Mom was busy bossing everyone around. When she hung up, she found Ian watching her closely. "Everly said not to rush back."

"Well, if you feel stressed about your mom, you can change your mind." He rubbed a hand over his jaw. "I wouldn't mind the excuse of not making it to the cemetery."

Brandy tilted her head, studying him. "I think you should go, or you might regret it."

"Yeah." He blew out a breath and glanced toward the window that overlooked the back parking lot. "You're right." His gaze moved to hers, his green eyes dark. "Ready?"

Fifteen

THE MOURNERS WERE GATHERED AROUND the gravesite by the time Ian and Brandy walked through the cemetery. Maybe only thirty people were attending this second portion, and Ian recognized some of Ella's relatives. An aunt and uncle, and a few cousins. Ella's family hadn't been large, and he knew one aunt lived on the East Coast, but he didn't see her among those gathered.

Ian was holding Brandy's hand again, and he wished they could be doing almost anything else but this. Facing Ella and Pete again was surreal, and it only brought back the emotional turmoil of the past. He didn't even have to mentally sort through memories of what had happened, what had been said, or all the paperwork and court hearings. His body felt weighed down—almost like he was carrying a physical weight. The warmth and assurance of Brandy's hand was what kept his feet moving forward, one step at a time.

As they neared the gathering, Ella headed straight for him. She'd reapplied her lipstick, and she smelled like she'd added another dose of expensive perfume. Before Ian could react, she enveloped him in a hug. "I was worried you'd ditched me," she said with an audible sniffle.

Ian had to release Brandy's hand if only to keep his balance. He patted Ella's back a couple of times, then tried to move out of her hold. But she clung to him like a life preserver in the middle of a lake.

"No one knew her like you did, Ian," Ella continued, her voice shaking.

Despite himself, Ian blinked back burning tears. Valerie had been an amazing woman, and she'd died much too young. Taking a steadying breath, he managed to extract himself from Ella. "She will be missed."

Ella grasped his arm, not giving him any space. Her eyes were reddened, so maybe her emotion had been genuine. "She missed *you*," Ella said. "So much. In her last days, she asked all about you, and I . . ." She dropped her gaze and wiped at her eyes. "I couldn't tell her anything about you because it was like you completely disappeared."

Ian didn't have an answer for that. They'd finalized the divorce, and he hadn't prioritized keeping in touch with an ex who'd ripped out his heart and stomped on it.

"Oh, Ian," she continued in a simpering tone, as if Brandy wasn't standing two feet away, and just a little farther, every funeral guest could probably hear them. "What happened to us? Why did we give up so easily? We should have gone to therapy. Or taken a long vacation. Something. Anything."

Ironically, these were the words he'd hoped to hear when things began to fall apart, but she wasn't interested. Not these exact words, but her pleading tone, her pretty face, her pouty lips. Unlike his early relationship with Ella, he could see past all that now. It was subtle, but it was there, in her eyes. The calculation. The desire to control. The addiction to being adored by another person.

He guessed that Pete no longer worshiped her in the way she wanted. So using his fondness for Valerie and dismissing the fact of her having betrayed *him*, she was working her magic.

Black magic, really.

"I'm very sorry about Valerie," he said, his words sounding thick in his throat. He extended his hand toward Brandy, and mercifully, she took it. "I didn't come to talk about what led to our divorce. I think we can let that be water under the bridge."

Finally, Ella's gaze cut to Brandy, acknowledging that she was there. "We'll talk later, honey. I know plenty of divorced couples who got back together. Maybe that will be *our* story. I'm still in shock over my mom's death, but I definitely know we have a lot to catch up on. I'll call you later tonight."

Ian held back a groan. "It's not necessary—"

"Oh, the service is about to start." Ella linked her arm through his.

He was so stunned that he didn't react at first. Then he firmly removed Ella's hand. "We'll meet you over there in a moment."

Ella's pout appeared, and she wiped at her eyes again, although there were no tears anymore. "All right, there's a place for you next to me. Don't be long." Then she moved close and kissed his cheek.

Ian could only stare after Ella as she walked toward the gathering. What was going on? Was she really acting like they were going to get back together? That a conversation was all he needed to come running back? Despite his answer being a firm no, he wondered what was going on with Pete. The man was sitting with the rest of the family before the casket covered in flowers.

"Did what just happened really happen?" Ian whispered to Brandy.

"It did." She tightened her hold on his hand. "It's like she doesn't even see me—or acknowledge that we're supposed to be together. Maybe it gives her more fuel to stoke whatever fire she's trying to start."

"Maybe," he ground out. "I'm going to block her number right now. I'm debating over Pete. He might need some self-help reference books."

"I'm sure he can find them on his own."

"You're right, and I'm just going back to the codependence thing by thinking I'll keep communication open with Pete." He released Brandy's hand and pulled out his phone. Then he blocked both contacts. "There."

"Good job," she whispered. "Took you long enough. I blocked everything about Brock the minute we broke up."

Ian grimaced.

"Too soon?"

He looked down at her and soaked in the sight of the woman who'd dropped everything to come with him. Her porcelain-blue eyes connected with his and her dimple had appeared. "Much too soon," he said. "But thank you anyway."

The words of the graveside service rumbled through a microphone, the sound system a bit dull and muted.

"Want to move closer?" Brandy asked.

They were still a half-dozen yards away from the main gathering and the empty seat that Ella had reserved for Ian. "No." He draped his arm around Brandy's shoulders and pulled her close. Nothing about his actions toward her were fake, not anymore.

She nestled against him, her arm going around his waist, as if it were the most natural movement for her. He didn't know if he heard one word from the reverend, and as soon as the man was finished, Ian led Brandy with him to the casket. They moved through the gathering, and heads turned to watch.

He stopped before the casket, not looking at anyone else, then placed the flowers on top that he'd brought. It was finished. His goodbye to Valerie was complete. He thought he'd feel empty, hollow, but all he felt was . . . peace.

This part of his life was completely over. He had plenty of regrets where Ella was concerned, but he'd never regret Valerie. He turned then, away from the casket, from Ella and Pete, and from the mourners. Hand in hand with Brandy, he walked across the cemetery, back to his truck. People were probably whispering and speculating, but he didn't care.

Once inside the truck, he started it up, not saying anything to Brandy.

She was quiet, though, seeming to know he needed to be immersed in his thoughts. They drove to the hotel, and after parking, he broke the silence. "Are you hungry or anything? We could change clothes and go eat. Or order something?"

"I'll order us something," Brandy said. "You have enough on your mind."

Ian nodded. He didn't even ask what she might order, because it really didn't matter.

They entered the hotel and headed down the hallway. Ian paused at his door. "Thank you, Brandy. For everything."

She didn't chastise him for thanking her so much. She simply nodded. "I'll let you know when the food arrives."

Once he was back in his hotel room, Duke was a welcome distraction. "Do you need to go for a walk?" he asked the dog.

The dog completely agreed. Ian changed his clothing, then headed out of the hotel, leaving his phone behind. The sky was nearly dark now, and the air had cooled. Perfect. He didn't know how long he was gone, but when he returned, there was a text from Brandy that the food had arrived. He texted back. *Sorry to miss your text, I took Duke for a walk.*

A knock sounded on his door a few minutes later.

Brandy stood there, a bag in hand. She had changed, too, and wore an oversized sweatshirt and short shorts. PJ shorts? He probably shouldn't be speculating about that. Her hair was pulled into a loose ponytail, and she'd scrubbed off her makeup. Did she know she was prettier without it? And her freckles were definitely cute.

"You might have to warm it up in the microwave." She held up the bag. "I hope you like Chinese food?"

"Chinese food sounds great," he said. "I'm actually feeling hungry now."

She handed over the bag, and he looked inside. There were three containers and a wrapped fortune cookie.

"What time should I be ready in the morning?" Brandy asked.

He had to think for a minute about that. "Anytime—do you want to get an early start or sleep in?"

"How about eight? I don't sleep too well in hotel rooms."

"Me neither."

Her blue eyes scanned his face, and he wished he knew what she was thinking about in that pretty head of hers.

"Well, have a good night," she said. "Text me if anything comes up."

Before she could step away, he grasped her hand.

Brandy's brows popped up.

"Stay," he said. "We can watch a brainless movie on TV. I'll share my fortune cookie."

She seemed to hesitate, and he released her hand. "No shenanigans," he added. "Fake or real. Promise."

Her cheek dimpled. "Do I get to choose the movie? Or are you going to go all ape and confiscate the remote?"

Ian lifted his free hand. "You can hog the remote all night if you want." Maybe that was too flirtatious?

Brandy laughed. "All right. Let me grab my phone, then I'll be right over."

Warmth shot through him. He was pleased—more than pleased.

He watched Brandy walk into her hotel room, then realized he was about to have company. He cleared his belongings off the king-sized bed, then straightened up the bathroom. Next, he popped the containers into the microwave. His stomach grumbled as if he hadn't eaten all day. By the time Brandy knocked on the door, he was ready.

Duke greeted her enthusiastically as she walked in. She took a minute to give the dog a good scratch-down.

"He missed you," Ian said.

Brandy kissed the top of Duke's head. "I missed him. Too bad he couldn't come with us to the cemetery. Maybe Ella would have been on her best behavior."

Ian dug the fork out of the bag, skipping over the chopsticks. "Ella doesn't have better behavior. She hasn't changed. Not even her mother's death could do that."

Brandy scanned his room. "Where should I sit?"

He nodded toward the bed. "Left side. I'll take the right."

Her blue eyes connected with his, filled with amusement. "You're assigning me a *side*?"

"You can take the right side, if you want. But the armchair is at the wrong angle to see the TV well."

She didn't respond, but crossed to the TV console and turned it on. Then she picked up the remote and browsed through movie selections.

"Do I dare guess? Are we watching a chick flick?"

Brandy's gaze cut to his. "They're called rom-coms, not chick flicks. Men should watch them with equal appreciation. There's a lot to be learned."

Ian smirked. "Oh yeah? Like what?"

"Just eat your Chinese food, Mr. Hudson, and let the master do the work."

Sixteen

THIS IS NICE, BRANDY DECIDED. No, not being on a bed with Ian—that was all platonic—but seeing him relaxed. And did she dare say, enjoying himself? She'd chosen an older romantic comedy—a classic, really—*Groundhog Day*. They'd both seen it, but Ian had seen it only once, and that was unacceptable to Brandy.

They were about halfway into the movie, and Brandy was pretty sure she was in a food coma from the extra Chinese she'd eaten with Ian. It had been good to see *him* eat, though, which made her feel like a mom—fussing over how much someone was eating in order to determine their happiness and well-being.

She smirked at her thoughts.

"What?"

Ian was way too observant sometimes.

"Nothing."

She felt his gaze on her, so she turned her head. Maybe her brain was mushy from the late hour and the very long day, but Ian looked very appealing, with his long legs stretched out on the bed. He wore faded jeans and a fitted Henley shirt, sleeves pushed up, that did nothing to disguise his excellent physique.

"You can't say 'nothing' when it's clearly something." His gaze scanned her as if he were appreciating her dressed-down appearance, too. The edge of his mouth lifted when their eyes connected, and she knew she was on the verge of blushing.

"I'm just having random thoughts," she said, her voice more whispery than she'd intended.

"Are we not watching the movie anymore?"

"We're still watching it, but I can't help it when my mind wanders for a second or two."

Ian turned over on his side, propping up on his elbow. "Well, I'm feeling left out of your thoughts."

Brandy scoffed. She mimicked his movement, turning toward him and propping up on her elbow.

Ian grinned, and Brandy's heart flipped over.

"Penny for your thoughts?" he ventured.

"I think inflation should make it like a hundred bucks for my thoughts."

"Done."

Brandy lifted a brow. "You're kind of a nut."

"I've been called worse." He winked.

Her face was heating up. "All right . . . I was thinking about how nice it was to see you relaxed. You know, after a crappy day. You ate food and now you're relaxing and laughing at a rom-com."

The dark green of his eyes lightened with amusement. "You were thinking about *me*?"

"It's hard not to when you're a foot away from me." Brandy turned over onto her back again and focused on the TV, because the longer she stared at Ian Hudson, the more attractive he grew.

"Three feet," he said, his voice seeming closer now.

She peeked at him. "What?"

"We're three feet apart."

Brandy turned her head more fully. Had he inched closer? "Three feet, one foot, it's all the same."

"Not the same." His gaze had shifted from humorous to something more intense. "Brandy . . ."

She found that she was holding her breath.

"Did I tell you how amazing you are and how grateful I am that you came with me?"

Brandy had no idea what was happening in the movie right now because all she could see or hear was Ian. "You told me like three hundred times."

His eyes crinkled at the corners. "I just want to make sure you know."

"I do know." The heat in her face spread to other parts of her body. There was much less than three feet between them, and when Ian reached across the space to smooth back hair from her face, her breathing nearly stopped.

"You're beautiful without makeup," he said in a voice so quiet, she wasn't sure she'd heard correctly. Then Ian's fingers skimmed the side of her face and rested against her neck in a featherlight touch. He slowly smoothed a finger over her strand of pearls. "I like your freckles."

"Thank you, I guess." No man had ever commented on them.

Ian's smile appeared. His barely-there stubble was dark against his face, and she wanted to touch his jaw, just to feel more of his warmth.

Her heart skipped a few beats at the thought.

The room's temperature had gone up several degrees at

least, and she wanted to move closer to him. Close the distance completely. Because if he wasn't going to kiss her, she was going to kiss him.

"Brandy..." he whispered again.

"Hmm?"

He didn't answer, though. His hand moved behind her neck as he shifted closer. His warm man scent invaded her senses, making her pulse skyrocket. Brandy reached up and touched his jaw. She'd been right. His whiskers scraped against her fingers, and his skin was warm.

This man was opposite of Brock in every way. Ian listened to her, he argued with her, he laughed with her, he expressed his gratitude, he was sincere, he didn't embellish the truth, and he'd let her see the vulnerability in his heart.

She'd seen Ian struggle through a difficult time, and she was happy she could be there for him. Yet kissing this man would be no casual thing. Brandy knew that with a certainty. Her heart had been broken into pieces, and she didn't know if she could handle any sort of one-night fling. The attraction between them was palpable, so what about tomorrow, or next week?

Her thoughts piled on top of each other, overriding what her heart was yearning for.

"I think we should wait," she whispered before Ian's lips could brush against hers. "It's been a crazy couple of days. I don't want to, um..."

"Regret anything?" he rasped.

"Exactly."

He hadn't moved back, hadn't given her space. His hand was still on her neck, his mouth only inches from hers. "Because kissing would take things beyond our fake relationship?"

"Way beyond." Brandy slowly ran her fingers along his jaw, then she withdrew her hand from his face, missing the warmth immediately.

"Okay." His agreement was simple, but somehow it twisted Brandy's heart.

Ian withdrew his touch, then edged away from her.

Brandy closed her eyes for a second, hoping she'd made the right decision. The bed shifted, and she opened her eyes. Was Ian getting up? No, he was rearranging the pillows, making a line of them between their bodies.

"What are you doing?"

"Making it easier to keep my distance," Ian said.

His tone was light, but Brandy felt the heaviness, too. He'd called her beautiful, and he'd almost kissed her, and he'd opened up to her . . . Yet instead of telling her to leave the room, he was simply putting pillows between them.

She didn't know if she should laugh or cry, or just kiss him anyway. Let tomorrow be its own hurdle.

When Ian lay back down, he linked his hands behind his head, which made his shirt ride up a few inches, exposing part of his lower stomach. So Brandy averted her gaze. She tried to focus on Bill Murray finally living through his most productive and perfect day—the day that would finally break the curse of reliving the same day over and over. Yet all she could think of was that she wouldn't mind reliving this day over and over with Ian. Well, minus the funeral. But she'd go on a road trip anytime, and she'd be fine adding a little mischief, too. Fake or real.

But she'd made her decision.

And tomorrow, she'd probably be happy about it. Hopefully.

Then, to her surprise, Ian reached over and grasped her hand. "Is this okay?"

"Is it fake?"

"No." His thumb slid slowly over her knuckles.

Brandy threaded their fingers together, his warm and strong. "Then it's okay."

Out of the corner of her eye, she saw him smile. Her heart was soaring again, and she smiled, too.

Bill Murray busied himself with carving an ice sculpture of his love interest. Andie MacDowell's character gazed at him with affection—acting well her part of being impressed by the man she thought was an empty shell of cynicism and sarcasm.

A knock on the hotel room door startled both of them.

Ian snapped his gaze to Brandy.

"Ella?" she whispered.

Panic flitted across his face. "Better not be."

Brandy paused the movie, and Ian climbed off the bed. He scrubbed a hand through his hair, then strode to the door. After looking through the peephole, he pulled the door open.

"Pete?"

Brandy moved off the bed as she heard the rumble of the other man's voice. She should go. Whatever they were going to talk about, they could do it without her. Maybe Ella wasn't far behind.

"Oh," Pete said as Brandy came into view. "You two really are together."

Ian had been right. Pete had hollows beneath his eyes.

"I should go," Brandy said in a quiet voice to Ian.

"No, stay." He paused and looked at her. "If you want."

So Brandy stayed.

Pete looked between the two of them. "Sorry to come over so late. I saw your truck in the parking lot when we were leaving the cemetery. I don't think Ella did, though. She was ranting about something, and she didn't mention it. Which she would have."

Ian folded his arms. "True. But why are *you* here?"

"I tried to text and call you." Pete held up his phone. "Apparently you blocked me."

"I did." Ian wasn't budging from the door frame. "I only came to pay my respects to Valerie's memory, not to get wrapped up in your new lives."

"That's fair." Pete shoved his hands in his pockets and looked down at the ground. "Look, I'm sorry. For everything. I should have never become involved with Ella. It was stupid of me, and I've regretted pretty much everything from the first day we crossed boundaries."

Ian didn't say anything for a long moment, but Brandy really wanted to head back to her room. Let these men work out what they needed to work out.

But then Pete turned his gaze to her, his eyes blinking rapidly. "Don't let this guy go. He's my best friend and the best man I've ever known. If I could reverse the last few years, I would, just to keep our friendship. Nothing has been harder in my life than knowing I hurt him."

Brandy's eyes welled. "I'm sorry that you're in this situation." She didn't know what else to say.

Pete took a step back, gave a short nod. "I'll not bother you anymore. Ella and I are over. She doesn't know it yet, but I'm telling her in the morning. I just can't do it anymore. Besides the fact that she's a difficult woman to tolerate, the guilt of what I've done has crippled everything else in my life. Ian, if you can ever forgive me, unblock my number and call me. I'd love to just hang out. Like we used to do before we started a business together."

Ian didn't move, didn't respond.

Pete lifted a hand in a half wave. "See you later, maybe."

Then he turned and walked away, shoulders hunched, head down.

Ian shut the door, then turned to face Brandy. After rubbing a hand over his face, he said, "What do you think about driving out right now? I can't risk Ella showing up here, too."

The pain and worry in Ian's eyes was clear. Even if they stayed the night, Brandy wouldn't be sleeping much. Besides, it would mean she could check on her mom a lot sooner. She stepped close to him and squeezed his hand, then lifted up on her toes to kiss his cheek. "Give me fifteen minutes to pack."

Seventeen

Brandy had brought Ian dinner three nights in a row, and he needed her to stop. Not because he didn't appreciate the meals—which were much better than anything he heated up from a can—but because he didn't want to be a charity case.

After returning in the middle of the night from the funeral the week before, they'd each gone their separate ways. Ian to his workshop and regular routine. Brandy to her job, her family, her friends. He had texted her the day after they'd returned to see how her mom was doing. Brandy's reply was brief and cheerful—that her mom didn't need surgery after all, but just had to wear a sling for a few days.

Then silence had dropped between them. Until three nights ago, when a meal showed up at his doorstep. By the time he'd reached the door, she'd disappeared down the trail to her place. He'd called her, but no answer. He'd texted her, and she'd put a thumbs-up on his message. If Brandy was trying to give him space by keeping her distance, she was doing an excellent job at it.

Or maybe the funeral trip had burned her out, and she

regretted going. Ella had been a lot to deal with, not to mention Pete's midnight confession. And . . . there was their almost kiss. Not that Ian regretted anything with Brandy, but now with some space between them, he understood why she'd turned him down. From her viewpoint, he was a mess, and she was still dealing with her own breakup stuff.

He could hear people at her cottage right now, and he smelled something cooking. Maybe this meant the meals would stop. Brandy was now back to her previous life filled with people. And Ian was back to his solo existence. Which he was happy with—or *had* been happy with, before her.

Duke whined at the door of the workshop, even though he knew better.

Ian had worked longer than usual today, and the dog was probably tired of being cooped up. Plus, he could certainly smell the cooking food.

"Let's get your dinner," he told the dog. "Then we'll go on a hike. You have to promise not to run over to Brandy's, though. She has company." And Ian didn't need another encounter with Steph. Although by the sound of voices floating over to his place, there was at least one man in the group. Maybe it was Austin? The other alternative didn't make Ian too happy—would Brandy be dating already?

Her relationship with Brock had been over for a few months, so maybe she was ready to move on? If she was, then Ian definitely wanted to know about it . . . Why? He admitted to himself that he was attracted to Brandy—in many ways. But it seemed she didn't return the feeling since she'd made herself scarce.

Unless he counted the meals.

Ian leashed up Duke to walk between the workshop and the cabin. He didn't trust the dog right now. Inside, he warmed up the leftovers from the night before—a chicken and rice dish. Duke ate the dog food quickly, then joined him at the table, eyes hopeful.

"Sorry, bud. No chicken for you. After your walk, I'll fix you a couple pieces of bacon." Ian rose to rinse out the dishes, then he again grabbed the leash.

They headed around the cabin and walked the trail that led to the summit of the hill, the same one Brandy had joined him on when she'd first arrived. The sun would set in about an hour, but Ian wasn't in any hurry. Walking back in the dark would be better anyway. Brandy's company would probably be gone.

Hiking up the hill burned his calves and thighs, but it felt good. The fresh air was cooling fast, which was refreshing. Everything about this location was peaceful, and now that he'd blocked Ella, it was like that chapter had closed for good. He'd decided to unblock Pete, and they'd had a couple of conversations over the past few days, but Ian wasn't going to renew their friendship back to square one. He'd wished Pete all the best and even recommended some podcasts and books. Pete had confirmed that he'd broken up with Ella, and truthfully, Ian was happy the man had seen some sense.

But he couldn't be involved, at least at this point, with anything ongoing in Pete's life. Whether or not the man was still with Ella. Too much had been betrayed. Pete had put in a furniture order, which Ian would fulfill, but after that, he had no plans to continue with anything.

Maybe in future years, things might change.

But as far as Ian was concerned, he was going to focus on his carpentry business.

Duke barked and ran ahead on the trail. "Found a squirrel, buddy?" The dog stopped and sniffed at a hole next to a scrubby bush.

"You're going to regret that if a snake lives there."

Duke barked again and blissfully continued up the trail.

Ian chuckled and followed. When they reached their usual boulder perch, his phone buzzed with a text. He pulled out his phone, surprised he had reception this far up. Brandy had texted him.

Hey, Ian, my mom wants me to invite you to Sunday brunch with my family. You can say no.

Ian stared at the words, unsure of the tone of Brandy's voice. Was she just passing on a message, *hoping* he'd say no? She could have just told her mom he couldn't come if that was the case. Why text him at all? And if Brandy did want him to come, but was playing it cool, did *he* want to go?

It sounded like a lot of . . . people. Would it be rude to ask who else was going?

He'd call her when he got back to the cabin. She was probably surrounded by her friends or family right now, and he didn't want his questions to be bandied about.

As the sun set, the valley below went from orange and gold to violet and blue. Duke sniffed everything in sight, then finally settled next to Ian. Only when dark finally covered the hills did he head back down the trail. The air had cooled significantly, so he pulled on the jacket he'd brought. He'd decided he'd bow out of the family brunch invitation. He wasn't sure he wanted to be peppered with questions from Lydia Kane or become part of her plot to get her daughter back to Everly Falls. As far as he was concerned, Brandy was perfect where she was.

As he neared his cabin, Duke had another burst of energy and sped up, sprinting into the clearing. "Duke, what's the rush?" he called out, then he saw why.

Brandy was sitting on his porch, wearing too little

clothing for the cooler evening. Shorts, flip-flops, a pale pink T-shirt—and the ever-present pearls. Her hair was down around her shoulders, blowing in the breeze. She stood as he approached, her arms wrapped about her torso, probably because of her goose bumps.

"Hey," she said, then bent to scratch the ecstatic dog.

Ian slowed his step. He didn't see any containers of food, so she hadn't brought leftovers. Besides, it was kind of late. And she needed to stop bringing over meals anyway. Surely she had other things to keep busy with.

When Brandy lifted her gaze, her blue eyes were troubled.

"Hey," Ian said back. "Party over?"

Her lips curved, but no smile reached her eyes. "Yeah. Were we too loud?"

"No." He tugged Duke away from being an attention hog. "Upstairs, boy." The dog miraculously obeyed and bounded up the stairs, then sat by the front door, panting.

"What's wrong?" Ian asked in a gentler tone, turning back to Brandy.

"Oh, I just wondered if you got my text." She tucked blowing hair behind her ear.

"I did."

Brandy tilted her head. "You can say no if you want, no pressure. It's just that my mom is shopping in the morning, so I wanted to give her an answer. You know, so she buys enough food."

"You've been feeding me all week," Ian said. "I'm going to have to start running with you if you keep it up, so I don't put on twenty pounds."

Brandy's cheeks pinked, and he was pleased with that for some reason. Yes, he knew her routine—Duke certainly kept him alerted to the fact that Brandy went running in the mornings around seven, sometimes along the trail that passed his cabin.

"It's hard to cook for one," she said casually. "And I'm not a huge fan of leftovers."

"So I'm like the garbage disposal?" There was her smile that he'd missed.

"Something like that."

"Well, thank you. I was worried you were feeling sorry for me or something."

"Not exactly," she hedged.

"As much as I appreciate it, you really don't have to keep dropping off food." He took a breath. Took a chance. "It would be nice to share the meal. I mean, in a completely neighborly way."

Her gaze scanned his face, and he found he didn't mind the scrutiny.

"I know you want your space," she said in a quiet voice.

"I do a lot of the time." He exhaled. "But not all of the time. And the space I need is from my former life and people I don't know. You're not included in that list."

Her dimple appeared.

"Come inside, you're freezing."

"I don't want to intrude," she said.

He didn't know what was going on, but her excuse sounded off. "If I'm inviting you, it's not intruding."

She bit her lip, indecision in her eyes.

"Here." He shrugged out of his jacket and set it across his shoulders. "I'll get it from you later."

"At the brunch?" Something in her eyes spoke of hope.

Did this mean she really did want him to come?

"Tell me about this brunch," Ian said. "Your text was a bit mysterious."

"Oh, um . . ." Brandy slid her arms into the sleeves of his

jacket, then she looked away, a far-off look in her eyes. "It's tradition in our family and some of my other relatives come. My aunt and uncle, and any cousins if they happen to be in town. Once in a while, a neighbor or friend." Her gaze shifted to his again. "Everly and Austin, and of course his daughter."

She drew in a breath. "I haven't been to one since before Brock and I split. And these brunches are the lifeblood for my mom and her sense of family unity. So I've felt bad about not going, but the last one I went to was when Brock first met Austin. From there, Brock decided that he still liked my sister."

"Ah." Ian rubbed the back of his neck. "So I'd be your buffer?"

"Yes."

"How can I say no to that?"

"You can't." Brandy's smile appeared then, tentative.

"Were all your dropped-off dinners meant to butter me up?"

Brandy lifted her hands, his jacket sleeves drowning her arms. "No, I swear. That was out of surplus food. My mom brought up the brunch when she visited this afternoon. She wanted to come to your cabin and invite you personally, but I talked her out of it. So you can thank me for that."

Ian grinned. "Thank you."

Her smile grew. "You're welcome."

The breeze stirred again, and this time Ian moved back the hair that was blowing against her cheek.

Brandy's blue gaze held his, and he wondered if she could hear his heart thumping. Even without seeing her this past week, she'd been in his thoughts, which had been much more pleasant than his usual ones. Maybe . . .

She stepped back, her smile still in place. "I should head

home. It's been a long day, and I need to call my mom." Her voice had a nervous edge to it.

"Are you sure you want me to come to the brunch?"

"Yes," Brandy said immediately. "Please."

What else could he say but yes? Maybe the time wasn't right to kiss this woman, but he could wait. He wasn't going anywhere.

Eighteen

BRANDY WASN'T SURE IF SHE was a fool or a glutton for punishment. Ian liked her. She could see it in his eyes. She could feel it in his casual touches. She could hear it in his words.

And *she* liked *him*.

That's what scared her. How could she bounce into another man's arms only three months after she thought she'd be marrying the love of her life?

Of course, she now knew Brock hadn't been the love of her life. He'd been the mistake of her life. Surely she'd learned plenty of lessons, though, which was why she didn't want to barrel into another relationship.

Even if it was Ian Hudson.

Inwardly, she sighed as they walked the path to her cottage. It would be futile to tell him she could walk on her own. He'd just follow her. Walking side by side was much better.

Duke trotted up ahead as usual, as if they were on a grand adventure. Brandy folded her arms, grateful for the warmth of Ian's jacket, although her legs were feeling pretty cold. She glanced over at him—he was watching Duke. Maybe he hadn't been about to kiss her—again. Maybe he was just touching her, being friendly? But she knew that wasn't the case.

And even though she'd been giving him space this week after the hard things he'd faced at the funeral, she'd thought about him constantly. What he was doing, what he was thinking, if he'd reconciled with Pete, if he'd recovered from seeing his ex-wife, if he missed Valerie, if he was eating good food . . .

She cared about this man. Bit by bit, it had just happened. Nothing was stopping her from turning their friendship into something else—well, nothing except for herself and her insecurities. With Brock, she'd been blindsided. And she wasn't about to let that happen again.

Yet she sensed the patience in Ian. He was going by her signals, her clues.

"Do you have a busy day tomorrow?" he asked. "Maybe we can go on a hike to one of the waterfalls."

She looked over at him, surprised. "Oh? I'm going to do some painting. I thought I'd sand the front door and paint it a color—blue or yellow. Maybe red?"

"Do you have a sander?"

"My sister brought up some sandpaper. It's not a big job."

"I have sanders," Ian said. "I could bring one over."

They'd reached the clearing, and there was really no reason for him to walk her to the door, so she stopped and faced him. "That would be great, but I'll probably be fine with the sandpaper."

"Brandy, it's not a problem." He shoved his hands in his pockets. Since she was wearing his jacket, his forearms were bare, and she noticed the goose bumps there. "Just text me what time you want to get started, and I'll bring it over. I can help you take the door off the hinges, too."

"Oh, I wasn't going to go to all that trouble." When she saw the surprise on his face, she added, "I guess you do things a little differently?"

"If you do it right the first time, then it lasts longer."

"Hmm."

He was waiting for her to answer, so she finally said, "All right. Bring the sander, and we'll take the door off its hinges. You can teach me carpentry 101."

Ian's smile warmed her through, and the butterflies were back. Both because standing beneath the moonlight with him made her feel like all the Brocks and Ellas were far, far away, and because spending part of the day tomorrow with Ian was something she definitely looked forward to.

"Thanks," she said, "you're nice to offer."

"It's not a problem," he said. "And if you're not too tired, we could still go on that hike. Duke would be ecstatic."

"I won't be too tired." She was smiling now. "Besides, anything for Duke."

Ian chuckled. "All right, I'll keep that in mind."

Another sigh rippled through her, and the breeze kicked up again, making goose bumps skitter along her body despite the oversized jacket.

"See you tomorrow," she said.

"See you tomorrow."

Before he could turn away, Brandy stepped close and kissed his cheek. She hadn't planned it, but she hadn't been able to stop, either. The stubble on his cheek was both rough and soft at the same time.

She lowered to her heels, but before she could analyze what she'd done or step away, Ian's hand slipped around her waist.

Neither of them moved for a moment as their gazes locked. He'd made the next move, but he was still waiting for her. And she was done making him wait. Brandy lifted her hands to his shoulders, then moved them behind his neck. That was an invitation Ian didn't turn down. He closed the distance between them, then his mouth found hers. Brandy sighed into his warmth and taste as he kissed her slowly, thoroughly, as if they had all the time in the world. And tonight, maybe they did. His lips were warm, soft, and well, Ian Hudson knew how to kiss a woman.

Brandy didn't remember ever being kissed with such intention or intensity. If she'd questioned whether to kiss him or not, those questions had all disappeared.

She moved her fingers into his hair and tugged him closer. Ian obliged, and his other arm snaked around her back, drawing her flush against his body. His chest was hard, his arms strong, and his mouth . . . exploring.

Was it possible to disintegrate in another person's arms? Brandy was grateful he was holding her up, because her knees had turned liquid. When his mouth moved to her jaw, his whiskers scraping against her face, fresh goose bumps rushed across her skin.

"Ian," she whispered, wondering if this was all real, if this was all happening.

"What?" he murmured against her neck, then pressed a kiss below her jaw.

"Nothing." She gave in to the warm shiver that traveled the length of her body.

He lifted his head, and she wanted to drag him back against her. But before she could, he cradled her face with his warm, callused hands. "Is this okay?" he asked, his voice low.

Her pulse thundered like a train rushing through her veins, and she was having trouble focusing. "It's okay."

The edge of his mouth lifted, then he kissed her again. Lighter this time. But lingering, as if he wanted to memorize every second of touching her. *She* certainly wasn't going to forget. The breeze stirred around them, and Duke gave a short bark, nudging against their legs.

Ian's chuckle was a low rumble. "He feels left out."

"You'll have to wait your turn, Duke," Brandy said.

Ian's hands moved down her arms, then threaded their fingers. "Now what?" he murmured.

"You tell me," Brandy said, locking gazes with him.

He released one of her hands and led her across the clearing to the cottage. "Well, I thought I'd walk you to your door like a proper gentleman, then in the morning, I'll come to your place with a sander."

They paused at her doorstep, and the yellow glow of her porch light deepened the green of Ian's eyes. She liked both options. "Does eight work?"

One of his eyebrows lifted. "On a Saturday? You don't mess around, do you?"

"I thought we could have breakfast together."

His smile appeared, and Brandy knew she wouldn't mind if he repeated his kissing.

"I'll be here. Do you want me to bring anything?"

"Your dog?"

"Ah, right." He winked. "Duke has all the luck."

"You have some, too."

"You're correct in that." He leaned close and kissed her again. One single, soft kiss. Then he stepped away, hands in his pockets as if he were trying to keep them to himself. "Good night, Brandy."

"Good night, Ian. Bye, Duke."

Ian walked backward for a few steps, his gaze locked on her, his half smile in place. He finally called for Duke to follow him, then he turned toward the path.

Brandy went into her cottage and watched out the window until they both disappeared into the trees. Putting her hand over her heart, she closed her eyes. What was happening? What had she done? How was it possible to be crushing on a man so hard?

Ian's kissing had been so gentle, yet intense, too. Did that mean he liked her more than being attracted to her?

She released a groan. What was she getting herself into? She pulled out her phone and texted Everly. *We kissed.*

Her phone rang, Everly's contact showing up. "Tell me everything," her sister said, "and don't leave out one detail."

Brandy laughed as she settled on the couch, then she sighed.

"That good, huh?"

"No details, but yes, it was toe-curling good," Brandy admitted. "I kissed his cheek first, but he definitely continued it. For a while."

"In your cottage? At his place? On a hike? Was the dog there?"

"Outside, and the dog was there, but that's all you're going to get."

Everly gave a dramatic sigh. "I'm happy for you, sis."

"You are? You don't think it's too soon?" Brandy asked in a softer voice. "Maybe this is a rebound crush? I don't think my heart can handle another roller coaster, and I don't know if I can invest in another person's well-being right now."

"Well . . . do you want this to be a fling? Or something more?"

"I have no idea." Brandy worried her lip. "Is that bad? I don't think Ian has a plan, either, although he's a lot more actualized about relationships than I am."

"What do you mean?"

"Just that he listens to podcasts and reads self-help books, so we've had some deep discussions."

"Ah, like the narcissist thing you told me about?"

"Yeah." Brandy pulled her legs up on the couch.

"You know what, Brandy? Maybe don't worry about the future so much. Enjoy the moment."

She exhaled. "Yeah, you're right. I just . . . really like him, but I also worry I'm living in a bubble up here. He doesn't have family, and I don't know if he has any friends besides those he's broken off with. Should a guy who's basically a loner be a red flag?"

Everly seemed to think about this. "At least there's a good reason for his extreme isolation. But I guess the question is if he's completely antisocial. You said he was interactive when your friends came over for a barbecue. He was more distant at the funeral, of course."

"Which is a given," Brandy agreed. "Maybe bringing him to the Sunday brunch will be a good test."

"He's coming?" Everly's excitement was plain in her voice.

"Yeah, he agreed." Brandy found herself smiling. That was a good sign, right? That Ian was reentering society, so to speak.

"He's going to get an earful of questions," Everly warned. "And there won't be any place to hide. Not if Mom has anything to do with it."

"True," Brandy said. "Tell Mom that Ian and I will do all the cleanup. I don't want her overworking herself."

"Okay," Everly said. "I'd rather cook anyway—Austin can be kind of fun in the kitchen."

"I don't need to hear it." Brandy teased, then she stifled a yawn. "Look, I should go. I think I'm going to take your advice, though. Just focus on a day at a time. Looking beyond that makes me feel a bit panicky."

"Good for you, sis. Love you."

When Brandy hung up with Everly, she moved through the cottage, turning off lights and double-checking locks. The place was so quiet, and even though she knew Ian's cabin wasn't far off, she felt lonely. More than she'd admit to her mom or sister. They'd been right, of course. Brandy was a people person. She'd never lived alone in her own place, and it was taking some getting used to. There were definitely pros and cons, but she'd had to stop herself multiple times a day from taking a work break and walking over to Ian's workshop.

Making him dinner had been something to look forward to. But now . . . with their kiss, would that change things? Would they hang out more? Would their relationship grow into something deeper?

After getting ready for bed, Brandy climbed beneath the covers and switched her phone to silent. That's when she noticed a text from an unknown number.

Brandy, this is Brock. I got a new number. I really need to talk to you. No one will tell me where you are, but please meet me. Just to talk. I've changed so many things, thanks to therapy and your wake-up call. I never loved Everly. Everything I told you about that relationship before I met you was true. My therapist said I simply had cold feet—I guess it's a thing for guys sometimes. Anyway, please don't block this number. Please forgive me. I'd love to meet soon. I'm a wreck without you.

Brandy didn't know when she'd started crying, but it was like she could hear the sound of Brock's voice as she read his words. She didn't need to ask herself if he was sincere—she knew he was. In *his* mind. From *his* perspective. "Cold feet" didn't give him the right to declare his feelings for her sister.

Besides, Brandy would never take him back. Meeting him would only reopen the painful wounds and insecurities. She wouldn't reply tonight, and she wouldn't block the new number. Not yet. Tomorrow, she'd think of something to say that would make him, and his apparent therapist, understand that things were permanently over.

Nineteen

THERE WAS NO SIGN OF life inside the cottage from where Ian stood on Brandy's porch. No lights on, no smell of breakfast cooking, no music, no other sounds. He knocked again, but was met with stark silence. Ian pulled out his phone and called her. It went straight to voicemail.

Frowning, he wondered if that meant she'd rejected his call—was she talking to someone else? Or maybe her phone was off?

"Brandy?" Ian called out. Duke barked, too.

Maybe he should sit on the porch and wait. She could have slept in and was now in the shower. So he settled on the rickety rocking chair on the porch next to where he'd left his tool bag and sander. The rocking chair must have been inside when he'd moved up here, because he didn't remember seeing it before Brandy moved in.

His gaze cut to where her car was parked. That meant she was here, right? Had she gone running? If she stuck to her routine, she'd be back by now. What if she got a late start? But would she really go running if there was work to do on the door? Maybe he could start on the sanding?

Ian rose to his feet and crossed to the door. It was locked, so there was no way he could take the door off its hinges unless he picked the lock. He sat back down, absently scratching Duke's head. The minutes dragged. Ten . . . Fifteen . . . He stood and paced the porch. Called Brandy again. Sent her another text.

Finally, he walked around the cottage, listening for anything. The curtains to what he assumed was the bedroom were closed. There was no light on in the bathroom, either—although she probably didn't need one in the daytime.

The longer Ian waited, the more worried he grew. He wished he had her mom's or sister's cell numbers. Maybe one of them picked her up and she'd forgotten to take her phone?

Duke barked, as if he were thinking the same things.

"Hey, bud." Ian gave the dog another scratch. He stepped up to the bedroom window and knocked. "Brandy?"

Nothing.

He headed around to the front of the house again. His gut only grew tighter. What if she was sick, or there was a true medical emergency? Finally, he dug out a couple of things from his tool bag, then stepped to the door. It took only seconds to get the lock open, and his heart pounded the whole time, his worry morphing to real concern.

"Brandy?" he called as he stepped inside. "Stay," he directed Duke, then pulled the door shut between them. Ian hadn't been inside the cottage since move-in day, and everything seemed to be as he remembered it, with a few added touches. A throw blanket and pillows had been added to the small couch. A couple of plants and a handful of books sat on the coffee table. The older-model refrigerator in the kitchen hummed.

There weren't any dishes in the sink, and the counters were cleared. The table was covered in stacks of paper, and nestled among everything sat a laptop, plugged into the wall.

"Brandy?" he said to the silent room.

The only thing left to do was check the bedroom. A short hallway led to a bathroom, which was empty, and the bedroom...

The door stood open, and it was instantly clear that Brandy was still in bed. Sleeping?

She was turned away from him, the covers pulled up to her shoulders.

His pulse raced as he approached the bed. Was she moving? Was she breathing? "Brandy?" he said in a quieter tone. "Are you sick?"

When her foot moved, relief rushed through him. "It's Ian. I came to check on you."

Brandy's arm appeared from under the covers and rested over her face. "Today's not a good day," she rasped.

The air left Ian's lungs. "Are you sick? I can get you something."

"No." This time her voice came out as a whisper. "I'm just going to sleep."

"Do you want me to start sanding the door?"

"No." She fell silent again.

Ian stood in the middle of the room, unsure of what to do. This was a side of Brandy he hadn't ever seen. Did she have depression? Was she in a depressive episode? Had something bad happened? Or was it just a rough night of sleep?

This morning was far from what he'd expected. After their shared kissing last night, he'd been eager to see her again. To see what their intimacy had meant—to her. He hadn't quite figured out what it might mean for him, but he at least knew she was a woman who surpassed Ella in every way possible. Which meant he wanted to get to know Brandy better, to find out where things might go, beyond their mutual attraction.

He stepped out of the room and shut the door quietly. He could make her something to eat, then leave her in peace. In the kitchen, he opened the fridge. The basics were there—and he could do the basics. He pulled out an egg carton, found a fry pan, then he was in business.

He tried to be as quiet as possible, but he assumed Brandy could hear the clinking. Unless she'd fallen back asleep? Once the eggs were bubbling away, he put bread in the toaster. Did she like butter and jam? Or the honey in the cupboard? He decided to spread the toast with jam since there were two kinds in the refrigerator.

He set the eggs on a plate, then poured a half glass of the orange juice he found. He didn't see a coffee maker, so the juice would have to do. Next, he quickly cleaned up, then headed to Brandy's bedroom door.

He knocked softly before opening it a few inches. She hadn't moved from her position, her arm still over her face.

"Made you some breakfast," he said to the silent room. "Call me if you feel like working on the door. My day is free."

Still, no answer.

He backed out and headed to the front door. He'd probably have to eventually answer to how he got inside, but he was relieved to know she wasn't dealing with a medical emergency.

As far as he was concerned, she could stay in bed and sleep all day. Maybe he'd make her lunch and dinner, too.

Still, his heart was heavy as he walked to his cabin, Duke following at his heels. He returned to his workshop, making sure his phone was on, and the volume turned up. Despite that, he checked it every fifteen or twenty minutes. By the time noon rolled around, he still hadn't heard a word from Brandy.

Had she gotten out of bed? Had she eaten anything?

Ian wasn't sure if he'd worried—or more accurately obsessed—over another person this much before. His grumbling stomach told him it was time to eat something, since he'd skipped breakfast himself. He headed into the cabin and made a quick sandwich—turkey, cheese, bacon, lettuce. Then he made a second sandwich and wrapped it up. When he walked out of the cabin, he stood on his porch for a long moment, gazing at the path that led through the trees. All was quiet, and he didn't like it.

"Come on, bud," Ian told Duke. "Let's go check on our neighbor."

Again he approached the silent cottage, then he knocked on the door. With no answer after several minutes, Ian tried the knob. It was still unlocked. He cracked open the door. All was quiet.

Questions raced through his head. Should he back off? Leave her be? Try to talk to her again? He told Duke to stay, then walked inside. The plate of food and glass of juice had been moved from the table. That was a good sign, in Ian's opinion. Brandy had at least come out of her bedroom.

He glanced down the hallway. The bedroom door was ajar, and he called out, "Brandy, it's Ian. I wanted to see if you need anything."

She didn't answer, so he continued to the door to peer inside.

Brandy was sitting up in bed, pillows stacked behind her. She was clutching the quilt to her chest. Her cheeks were tear-stained, and her eyes puffy from crying.

"Hey," he whispered.

"Thank you for making me breakfast," Brandy said in a hoarse voice. "Today's not a good day for anything. Can I take a rain check on the door?"

"Of course." He pushed the bedroom door open wider

and leaned against the frame. "Do you want some lunch? I brought you my famous turkey sandwich."

Her eyes welled with more tears, and she wiped at her cheeks with a wadded tissue. "Famous, huh?"

"Well, maybe according to me and Duke, but it's pretty good."

Brandy gave a weak smile, but she kept her gaze lowered.

"Tell me what you need, Brandy," he said in a gentle tone. "I can head into town and pick up anything."

She gripped the quilt tighter. "I'm fine."

Ian released a slow breath. She was clearly *not* fine. "Do you want me to call anyone? Maybe your sister?"

Brandy shook her head, then reached for another tissue from the box on the bedside table. She folded it in half, then half again. "I'll call her later. I don't need her rushing up here." She sniffled. "It's better that I just get through today. Tomorrow will be better."

Ian was pretty sure she was trying to convince herself more than him. "Meanwhile, you should eat something. If you don't like turkey, I can come up with something else. Any preferences?"

It was then that her blue eyes lifted and looked at him for the first time since he'd entered. "You really don't have to."

"Too late." He held up the sandwich.

The indecision was plain in her eyes, but it wasn't a no. Yet.

"Here, try it. If you don't like it, Duke will happily eat what's left." He crossed to the bed and held out the wrapped sandwich. After a pause, she reached for it.

"Water bottle?" he asked, knowing there were some in her fridge.

She nodded. "Sure. Thanks."

"Be right back." Ian strode to the kitchen and pulled out two water bottles from the fridge. Then he returned to the bedroom. There wasn't anywhere to sit in the small space except for the bed. So Ian gave her one of the water bottles, then sat on the corner farthest from Brandy.

She slowly unwrapped the sandwich, then took a tentative bite. After she chewed and swallowed, she said, "It's decent."

"Only decent?" Ian slapped a hand over his heart. "That took years to perfect."

Brandy wrinkled her nose, but her eyes had brightened. "It's literally four things plus mayo."

"Okay, fine," Ian teased. "What would make it better?"

"Tomatoes."

"I was fresh out, but that will be the first thing on my shopping list next time I go." He pulled out his phone and made a show of typing it into the Notes app.

"Funny," Brandy deadpanned.

"I'm serious." Ian turned his phone so she could see his grocery list. Right beneath ice cream and bread, he'd written *tomatoes.*

Brandy rolled her eyes, then took another bite. Ian opened the second water bottle and drank from it.

"If you're going to be so picky, you need to give me a heads-up on what you want for dinner," he said. "I can run to the store this afternoon."

"I have enough food here, and tomorrow is my mom's brunch."

"You still going?" This gave him hope, although he didn't know if that meant he was still invited.

Brandy set the sandwich aside and picked at a thread on the quilt. "Yeah. I'm still going, and you're still invited."

Her tone was melancholy, but Ian was glad she wasn't canceling his invite. He might have been hesitant at first, but if it eased whatever was going on in Brandy's mind, he was happy to attend.

"What should I wear?" he asked, half-kidding.

Her gaze lifted again. "Jeans are fine. My mom will get gussied up, but everyone else comes casual."

Her voice was sounding normal now, and the tears were no longer falling.

"Okay."

Silence stretched between them, and Brandy drank from the water bottle. Then she turned on her side, facing him. "Thanks for the food."

"You mean the sandwich you ate two bites of?"

A smile played on her face.

Then she patted the space next to her.

Ian's heart skipped a couple of beats. Then he tugged off his shoes and moved up by her. She nestled against his chest and he looped an arm about her.

"This better?" he rumbled.

She nodded against his chest, and he thanked whichever lucky star he'd ever wished upon. He smoothed her hair from her face, then continued to thread his fingers through the blonde strands. "So the kiss last night wasn't horrible?"

She gave a small laugh. "No."

"That's good."

Brandy moved her hand up his chest, then rested it on his neck. His pulse beat steady beneath her soft fingers. "Brock texted me from a new number last night."

Ian's pulse jumped. "What did he say?"

"That he wants to reconcile, that he made a big mistake, that he's in therapy."

When she stopped speaking and didn't give her opinion

or the outcome, questions piled up in Ian's mind. Was she going to take him back? No, she wouldn't be curled up next to him if she was . . . right?

"What did you say?" he had to ask.

Brandy sighed, then lifted her head to meet his gaze.

Her eyes were lighter now and less worried. "I lay awake half the night. Then this morning, I texted him back and told him I'd moved on and that I was dating someone. I wished him the best and asked him not to contact me again. Then I blocked his number for good measure."

That was all good, right? But why had she been crying so much?

A line formed between her eyes. "I sort of lied to Brock. I mean, I've tried to move on, but I still feel like a mess. And I'm not technically dating you."

"We *could* be dating," Ian ventured. "I mean, we've kissed, more than once. And we're in bed together right now."

Brandy's face pinked, and he couldn't stop his grin.

She swatted his chest. "I'm going to kick you out if you don't take that back."

"I'm not going to take it back," he said, teasing. His tone sobered. "Brandy . . . I'm not a one-night-stand type of guy. I wouldn't have kissed you if I didn't want to date you."

Brandy's dimple appeared. "But I kissed you first."

"True . . ." He leaned close and pressed his mouth against that dimple of hers. "And I kissed you second."

"True," she echoed.

Her hand shifted to behind his neck. He didn't need the encouragement because he was all in. He moved his free hand across her hip, then up her back, drawing her closer. Her curves fit perfectly against the hard planes of his body.

"Brandy," he whispered.

"Hmm?"

"I'm sorry you had a rough morning," he said. "It gets easier with time."

She buried her face in his neck and held him tight as he traced his fingers up and down her back.

"I think you'd better take me on a date so I'm not a liar," she murmured.

"Okay." Ian moved one of his hands to her shoulder, tangling his fingers in her hair. "Tonight? Six o'clock, dinner at my cabin?"

"More turkey sandwiches?"

Twenty

DINNER WITH IAN LAST NIGHT had been fun, and the hours had passed without Brandy realizing it. They'd played some zany card game, then they went through his photo albums. His dad had not only been a carpenter, but also an amateur photographer. The albums of his dad's photography were something that Ian had put together after his death, as a tribute.

It had been both sweet and heartbreaking at the same time.

Ian had so many regrets—heavy regrets, really. About his strained relationship with his father before his death, about his choices with Ella, and his broken friendship with Pete. Brandy hadn't known really what to tell him to make him feel better, so she'd just listened. Maybe that had helped?

Time would tell, she guessed.

Right now, she was waiting for Ian to drive down the road to the cottage. They were taking his truck to her mom's because they'd decided to bring Duke. Her mom had a fenced backyard, and Duke could play there. Besides, Everly said that Austin's daughter would love to play with him.

So win-win?

Yet why were the butterflies in her stomach buzzing about in a horde of anticipation? On one hand, maybe it was because she felt like she was going back in time. Attending Mom's brunch, but this time with a different man. A man who wouldn't suddenly decide her sister was the preferred sister. No, that wouldn't be an issue . . . It was just that she hoped she'd be stronger now. Less triggered.

The rumble of the truck's engine sounded, and Brandy grabbed her phone, then headed outside. She could do this. Ian would be with her the entire time.

He parked and got out.

"You don't have to get out," she said. But he walked around the truck and opened the door for her.

"Thanks," she added.

"How are you?" he asked, his green eyes focused on her.

"Fine."

Her tone must not have been convincing because he said, "Come here."

She stepped into his arms, and when he pulled her close, she let her eyes close. How was it that Ian knew exactly what she needed? She loved his fresh-showered smell, the soft cotton of his button-down, and the steady beat of his heart. How could a woman—Ella, specifically—be so cruel to him?

"Thanks."

"Mm-hmm." He kissed the top of her head, and she released him.

The longer she stood here, the easier it would be to cancel on her mother. And that would be a whole dramatic affair. Ian handed her into the truck, even though she could have managed just fine on her own.

Duke pushed his head between the seats, panting. "Hello, buddy." She gave him a good scratch as Ian walked around to the driver's side.

When he climbed in, he started the engine, then looked over at her. "Ready?"

"Yeah."

He gave a short nod, then pulled onto the road. They didn't talk much as they drove, and Brandy concentrated on scratching Duke, who didn't mind at all.

As they neared Everly Falls, Brandy gave Ian directions to her mom's place. She lived in an older neighborhood. They parked behind another truck—Austin's white one.

"Looks like Everly and Austin are already here."

A couple of other cars were parked across the street, but Brandy didn't recognize them. Ian again opened her door, then offered his hand. She grasped it to climb out. Next, he opened the door for Duke and slipped on his leash, then grabbed a couple of dog toys.

"Come on, I'll show you the backyard," she said.

They headed toward the gate that led to the backyard. Once Duke was off his leash, he joyfully ran to each bush and blade of grass, sniffing as if he were in heaven.

"Dog life is awesome," Brandy commented as she watched Duke. Her mom would probably see them in the backyard at any minute, so she didn't take Ian's hand. She didn't want a million questions.

"Oh, and I need to tell you that I told my sister we're, uh, involved," Brandy said. "But my mom doesn't know anything, and it would probably be good if she didn't at this point."

"Got it." Ian slipped his hands into his pockets. "So no making out on your mom's couch?"

Brandy scoffed. "As if." But her face had warmed anyway.

Duke caught sight of a buzzing fly and leapt for it.

"What does your sister think?" Ian ventured. "About me?"

Brandy met his serious gaze. His voice was light, but she'd heard the sincere question in his tone. "She approves."

Ian's eyes crinkled at the corners. "Cool."

Brandy really wanted to kiss him, right here, right now. But the large dining room window prevented her from taking such a risk. Besides, the sliding glass doors on the deck had just opened, and her mom's voice sailed out. "Brandy! You're here! Why didn't you come in the front door with your guest? He's going to think we're chumps."

"Mom, no one says 'chumps' anymore." Brandy walked toward the back deck. "We've got Duke with us, and we didn't want to bring him through the house."

At the sound of his name, Duke bounded over to Brandy. "You're a good boy, aren't you?" she told the dog.

"Hi, Duke," a younger voice said from the open sliding glass door.

Brandy looked over to see Jessica, Austin's seven-year-old daughter. Her brown hair was done up in two braids, and her dark brown eyes were a mirror image of her father's.

"Do you want to pet him?" Brandy asked. "He's very friendly."

Austin appeared behind Jessica, and together they walked outside.

"Sit, Duke," Brandy said. "Good boy."

"He's big." Jessica's voice held trepidation.

"Golden retrievers are super nice," she said. "Even though he's big, he's like a dopey teddy bear."

"Agreed," Ian filled in.

Everly came outside, too, and grasped Austin's hand. The pair was rarely apart when in the same location. Brandy was thrilled her sister had found her man, at last, after what Brock had put her through.

Jessica reached out a hand and touched Duke's ear. "His

ear is so soft."

"Sure is," Brandy agreed.

Jessica grew braver and began to scratch the dog's back.

"He loves to play catch with kids," Ian said. "If you throw this tennis ball, he'll bring it back."

"Really?" Jessica took the tennis ball and threw it. Although it went only about five yards, Duke sprinted to the ball, passed it, then rounded back. He scooped up the ball in his mouth and ran toward Jessica.

She leapt back, startled.

Ian chuckled. "Now, tell the dog 'release,' and he'll give it to you. Then you can throw it again."

"Release," Jessica said in her small voice.

Duke dropped the ball into her hand.

"Ew. It's wet."

All the adults laughed. "Yeah, you'll have to wash your hands later," Ian said. "Throw it again."

So Jessica did. Over and over. Her squeals and laughter eased the tension that had built up in Brandy over coming to this brunch.

Her mom remained on the porch, her hands on her hips, her gaze focused like a laser on Brandy. It was clear she had questions, probably about Ian.

"Oh, someone's at the door," Mom said to no one in particular. She hurried into the house while the rest of them watched Jessica throw the ball.

Brandy kept her arms folded so she wouldn't reach for Ian's hand. The more she was around him, the more she liked him. His grin at Jessica's antics was absolutely adorable. She wondered idly what he thought of becoming a dad someday. Especially after his rocky relationship with his own father. Yet seeing him now, Brandy had plenty of confirmation that Ian was very patient with kids.

She really shouldn't be letting her thoughts run wild.

"Come inside, everyone. Aunt Janice and Uncle Stanley are already here," her mother called. "Unless you're planning on eating outside."

That was Mom's code for eating inside—where she'd set the table.

"Can I stay outside and play with Duke?" Jessica asked her dad. "I'm not hungry."

Austin glanced at Everly, then said to his daughter, "It's not polite to turn down food when you've been invited for a meal. Eat what you can, then in a little bit we can come back out."

Jessica's face scrunched, and Everly said, "Maybe Ian will let us feed something to Duke?"

Brandy was about to cut off that idea, when Ian said, "Sure. He can have a treat—if there's bacon or something like that." His gaze had locked on to Jessica. "But you'll have to finish your meal first."

Her smile appeared. "Okay." With that, she skipped to the deck and ran up the stairs.

"Well, that was easy." Austin chuckled. "Thanks, man."

"Not a problem," Ian said.

Once they were inside, introductions were made with Aunt Janice and Uncle Stanley, who were regulars at Mom's brunches. Thankfully, they were the only extra relatives attending. It would make the questions less intense.

Brandy sat between Everly and Ian. Her mom took her usual place at the head of the table, which had been set with her wedding china. Several covered dishes of food had been set on the table, and Brandy could smell breakfast fixings. Jars of syrup, bowls of preserves, and platters of butter dotted the table.

"A toast," Mom declared, lifting her glass of orange

juice.

Everyone looked a bit confused, but went ahead and picked up their glasses of either milk or juice.

"To Brandy," Mom continued. "Returning to Everly Falls to rejoin life."

Brandy stared at her mom, who seemed oblivious about how her toast had sounded. Everyone clinked glasses with the person next to them, but Brandy set her glass down. "Mom . . . I'm not coming back to Everly Falls, at least not for a while."

Her mom's eyes narrowed. "You said two or three weeks. It's been more than that now."

She didn't really want to discuss this in front of the whole family. "I said *maybe* two or three weeks. I'm playing it by ear."

Mom's mouth pursed into a line, and her gaze shifted to Ian.

Brandy frowned and looked at him, but he had the deer-in-the-headlights look on his face. "Like I said, Mrs. Kane, I'm the wrong person to talk Brandy into moving. I love it up in the hills."

"But you're a *man*, and you're independently wealthy." Mom waved a hand. "You've chosen to live alone."

The entire table had gone quiet.

"That's true," Ian conceded.

Brandy's stomach felt as hard as a rock. They hadn't even taken one bite of food and there was a family argument.

"Should we eat?" Everly said in a cheerful tone. "Smells amazing, Mom."

Her mom's tight expression eased a sliver. "Yes, let's eat." But the daggered gaze she threw at Brandy was clearly "we're not finished with this conversation." Obviously, her mom had held on to the three-week estimation with a lot more veracity than she should have.

Brandy hid a sigh and scooped some hash browns onto her plate when Everly handed them over. The conversation buzzed about her, with Austin talking to Uncle Stanley about his fishing trip, and Everly and Jessica chatting about some new Barbie movie.

Aunt Janice was telling Mom about a sale on calico fabric.

Brandy took a bite of her food, although her appetite had gone to nil. Why did coming home to her mom's make her feel like a teenager again?

"You okay?" Ian whispered.

It was then she realized her eyes had filled with tears. She blinked them back before they could fall. "Yeah."

Ian reached for her hand under the table. He linked their fingers, then picked up his fork with his left hand. Brandy knew he was right-handed, but somehow, he'd made the switch in order to comfort her.

She wanted to cry for a different reason now.

"He asked about Brandy, of course," Aunt Janice said, her voice a notch above the rest.

Brandy snapped her gaze to Mom and Janice. "Who are you talking about?"

Twenty-One

THE EDGE TO BRANDY'S VOICE put Ian immediately on alert. He knew she was stressed about coming in the first place, but he hadn't expected her mom to bring up Brandy's move in front of the entire family. Lydia Kane was a persistent woman.

Now, the table went quiet again, and Brandy's aunt looked over at her.

"Well, dear, I ran into Brock." Janice was a round-faced woman with large eyes and spidery eyelashes. "Don't worry, I didn't tell him where you're living. Your mom swore us to secrecy."

"That's right." Uncle Stanley nodded, then took another bite of a pancake.

Brandy's grip had tightened on Ian's hand. He'd be glad when this meal was over. It seemed that her family insisted on bringing up land-mine topics.

"Did he ask where I lived?" Brandy asked in a stiff voice.

On the other side of her, Everly put a hand on Brandy's shoulder.

"Not in so many words." Janice's gaze flicked to her

husband's as if for confirmation.

Stanley cleared his throat and dabbed at his mouth. "He was friendly, as usual. Asked after us, then said he was hoping to see more of the family soon."

Janice gave a vigorous nod.

"What else?" Brandy prompted.

"He said . . ." Janice stopped and glanced at Lydia. "He said he missed seeing us at the family brunch. And he asked if we'd talked to Brandy lately. Asked how she was doing and if she liked her new place."

Stanley gave a quick shake of his head. "We thought he knew where you lived, with a comment like that. We still didn't say anything."

"It was a close call, though," Janice said with a nervous smile.

Next to Ian, Brandy released a slow breath.

"Where Brandy lives or what she does isn't Brock's business," Everly said. "Next time you see him, don't give him *any* information about our family."

"Of course not," Janice murmured, but guilt flashed across her face.

"Well, that's that," Lydia said in a bright voice. "We can't change the past, can we?" Her gaze moved to Brandy's. "We can only focus on the future. What are everyone's plans next weekend? It's the fall festival at the park, you know. Is your mom still coming, Austin?"

"She sure is," Austin said. "She's planning on running a craft booth."

"And I'm going to help!" Jessica pronounced.

Ian was grateful for the change in conversation, but he could tell Brandy wasn't too happy. She hadn't eaten more than a couple of bites, and now she was staring at her plate.

"What do you need?" he asked in a quiet voice.

"I need . . . some space." She set her crumpled napkin on the table, then told him in a lowered voice, "I'll be in the backyard with Duke. Let me know when it's time to clean up."

Before Ian could respond, Brandy stood. "I'm going to check on the dog," she said to the table in general.

"Can I come?" Jessica popped up from her chair.

"When you're finished eating," Austin said.

Jessica's face fell, but Ian distracted her by telling her about some of Duke's adventures. If Brandy needed some time to herself, then he'd try to give that to her. As the conversations continued around the table, Ian felt Lydia's gaze on him more than once. He sensed she wanted to talk to him without Brandy around. If it was about encouraging her to move back to Everly Falls, his answer would be the same.

Austin asked him about his carpentry business and expressed interest in checking out the workshop. "Anytime," Ian told him. "Just send me a text first." On that note, they exchanged phone numbers.

When people finished eating, Ian stood and began to clear the plates.

"You don't need to clean up," Lydia said immediately. "You're our guest."

"It's no problem, Lydia," he said, carrying the plates to the kitchen.

Jessica was finally allowed to go play with Duke, and Everly and Austin started on the dishes as Ian finished clearing the table. Through the windows, he could see Brandy and Jessica throwing the tennis ball for Duke. Brandy smiled at something Jessica said, and relief shot through Ian. Maybe she was fine. They'd gotten through the initial part of this, right? Brock had been discussed. The worst had to be over.

"Ian, can I speak with you?" Lydia said, coming into the kitchen.

He glanced over at her, then at the mess that still needed to be cleaned up.

"Go ahead," Everly said. "We've got this."

Ian was about to protest, but she added, "We owe you for bringing your dog. Jessica's in heaven."

So Ian followed Lydia to the living room. Apparently, Janice and Stanley had already left.

"Look." Lydia faced him with her arms folded, her painted brows arched high. "I don't know what's going on with you and Brandy, but she's in a fragile state. She was in a serious relationship with Brock, and now she's turning to *you* instead of coming home where she belongs. I can see the way she looks at you and is depending on you."

Ian opened his mouth, then closed it. Should he reply? Or just listen?

Lydia pressed on. "Maybe if circumstances were different, I'd feel differently. But they're not. I'm not asking you anymore, I'm *telling* you . . . Brandy needs to come home where I can make sure she's all right. I don't need her becoming attached at the hip with another man who's practically a stranger."

"I understand your concern," Ian said, keeping his tone as even as possible. "But Brandy is a grown woman. Her mind is sound. I agree that she's still struggling with the betrayal by Brock, but that doesn't mean she can't live on her own, and that we can't be friends."

"You don't get it," Lydia said. "It's not healthy for Brandy to jump into another relationship so soon."

Ian lifted a hand. "We're not in a relationship, ma'am. Like I said, we're *friends.*"

Lydia pressed her lips together and tilted her head. "I wasn't born yesterday. I see the way you look at her, and I see the way she looks at you. Feelings have started between the two of you, and the last thing I'm going to allow is for my daughter to be hurt again."

He exhaled as his mind caught up to all that Lydia was implying. How did Brandy look at him? Should it worry him? Scare him off? No . . . if anything, he wanted to explore those feelings. Spend more time with Brandy. Figure out what came next between them. "I'm not going to hurt your daughter."

"The only way you can promise that is by staying away from her."

Ian stared at the woman and her blue eyes that were darker than Brandy's. "What if staying away from her is what will hurt her the most?"

Lydia's eyes slitted. "You have a very high opinion of yourself."

He folded his arms. This conversation was taking a hard detour. "I care about Brandy, Lydia. We have a lot in common and a deep connection. I can't predict the future, but I'm no Brock. I'm not going to betray your daughter's trust. Right now, Brandy needs her family to have a little faith in her. She doesn't need to be treated like one of your china plates. She needs to make her own decisions, and that includes where and how she wants to live."

Lydia scoffed. "I've been letting her make those decisions, and look where it's gotten her. A broken engagement and a broken heart."

"You wanted her to stay with Brock?"

"No." Lydia's face flushed. "That's not what I meant. But two wrongs don't make a right."

"The second wrong being . . .?"

"Brandy living isolated up in the hills."

"I'm there, and Duke. Town is only a twenty-minute drive."

Lydia closed her eyes.

In that moment, Ian saw a worried mother. As persistent and intrusive as she might be, at the heart of it all, she was just concerned about her daughter.

"Lydia," he continued in a quieter tone. "I won't let anything happen to Brandy. As long as she wants to live in that cottage, I'll watch out for her."

"Ian?" someone called from the kitchen—it was Brandy's voice.

Lydia pressed her lips together and turned away, so Ian headed into the kitchen.

"Where were you?" Brandy asked, her eyes full of questions that she could probably answer. Everly and Austin had finished the dishes and were now outside with Duke and Jessica.

"Chatting with your mom." He moved to grab a washcloth, then started wiping down the counters.

"Oh?" Brandy's gaze followed him as he worked. "How did that go?"

Ian glanced toward the living room, then nodded his head, hoping to signal to her that her mom could probably overhear them. "Great."

Brandy's mouth quirked. "All right, then." She stepped close to him and put her hand on his arm. "Thanks for coming."

"No problem," he said in a lowered voice, and he meant it.

"Thanks for cleaning up, too."

Ian smiled, and Brandy smiled back. It was good to see her relaxed again. Maybe being outside with the dog and

Jessica had been just what she needed.

"You're very welcome," he murmured, drawing back because he was sure Lydia was going to come around the corner at any second, and he was sorely tempted to pull Brandy into his arms.

A line appeared between her brows. "What did my mom say to you?"

"Uh, we can talk later." Ian rinsed out the washcloth in the sink, then wrung it out.

"Mom," Brandy called.

"Yes, dear?" Lydia came around the corner, a bright smile on her face.

"You don't need to go behind my back and talk to Ian about me moving home."

Lydia blinked her blue eyes innocently. "We both want what's best for you, dear."

Ian clenched his jaw. Lydia Kane was something else.

"And that is . . .?" Brandy prompted.

Here it came . . .

"You know you're not ready for another relationship," Lydia said. "Ian here is a nice man, but you're so isolated up there—and I think you've become too attached to someone who—"

"Mom." Brandy held up her hand. "Stop right there. Ian is an amazing guy, and we're friends. That's all you need to know. I'm fine in the hills. It's different, yes, but I'm getting through what I need to get through. Ian's helping me with some things, too."

"Like what?" Lydia set her hands on her hips. "You know you can call me anytime. I can even stay with you if you insist on living at the cottage."

"No, Mom," Brandy said. "Thanks for offering, but like

I've told you multiple times, I need to do this for myself. This isn't for you, for Everly, or even to get over Brock. I'm over him, and I'm done with him. But that doesn't mean I want to be faced with his memory every single day. I deserve a break from all that."

Lydia sighed. "Yes, of course you do."

"And Ian . . . well, you'll just have to get used to him being in my life." She looked over at him, questions back in her eyes. "We're good friends."

There was that *friend* word again, but Ian would stick with it. Then Brandy moved to his side and grasped his hand—a bold move in front of Lydia, who blinked a couple of times.

"I know you think I'm rebounding, Mom," Brandy said in a gentle tone. "But I'm not. You have to trust me a little."

Ian's pulse seemed to have skyrocketed.

Lydia took a shaky breath. "I do trust you, sweetheart, I just . . ."

"No justs or buts or shoulds." She tugged Ian by the hand toward the sliding glass door. "We're going to hang out for a bit in the yard, then I'm going back to the cottage."

Twenty-Two

"I THINK YOU MADE YOUR mom speechless," Ian said as they headed out of Everly Falls. Not only had Brandy held his hand in front of her mom, but she'd made it clear that she wasn't returning home anytime soon.

"That's impossible," Brandy said in a light tone. "Lydia Kane is never speechless. I just surprised her—although I don't think she was entirely surprised. She knew I was bringing you."

"True, but she didn't know there was something going on between us." He smiled because Brandy's gaze snapped to his.

"And that would be..."

He reached for her hand and tugged it onto his lap. "You tell me."

Brandy leaned her head against his shoulder. "Can it be enough that I think you're an amazing guy and it's kind of fun to kiss you?"

Ian chuckled, although his neck had warmed up, and he wanted to pull her closer. But he should focus on driving them safely to their destination. "Those things are definitely enough. We aren't on any time crunch now that you broke the news to your mom."

Brandy sighed at that. "I really don't know how long I'll stay in the cottage, but I don't want my mom counting the days, either."

Ian ran his thumb over her fingers. "Yeah, I get it. There isn't really a time limit on healing and moving on."

She squeezed his hand. "Oh, I've definitely moved on."

"Good to hear." Ian liked this. Their open talks. Spending time together. After many months of fighting his own way through his mess, having someone to share the small things with felt great.

As they rounded the final bend that brought the cottage into view, Brandy drew in a breath. At that same moment, Ian spotted a black sports car parked near the cottage. A man leaned against it, arms folded, his gaze locked on their approaching truck.

"It's Brock," Brandy said in a half whisper, straightening. "He's found me."

Ian let off the gas pedal, slowing the truck. "Do you want me to tell him to leave while you stay in the truck?"

"No," she said. "I don't know . . . I just can't believe he found me. Why is he here? I told him to leave me alone."

"Brandy, I can talk to him." Ian slowed the truck even more. "It will send a strong message. We could even call the cops."

"No," she said in a breathless tone. "This meeting is inevitable. Maybe he'll finally move on if I tell him in person."

Ian wasn't too sure about that. The blond man up ahead had fully turned to face them. His dark jeans were paired with a T-shirt that clearly showed this man liked to spend time in the gym. His aviator sunglasses mirrored the approaching truck. Ian pulled up right next to the black sports car, giving it a fine coating of dust.

"I need to do this, Ian. You can stick around, but don't interfere, okay?"

"Okay," Ian said, although he wasn't sure if he could honor her request.

Brandy popped open the door as soon as the truck stopped.

Ian turned off the engine. "Stay here, Duke," he said, then climbed out.

Brandy walked around the front of the truck and stopped several feet away from Brock.

"Who's this?" Brock asked, clearly meaning Ian, but not deigning to look at him.

"Ian Hudson," he cut in.

"What are you doing here, Brock?" Brandy said, her tone sharp. "I told you not to contact me."

Brock pulled off his sunglasses and looked first at Ian, then at Brandy. "Can we talk somewhere private?"

"There's nothing to say." Brandy folded her arms. "We've talked in enough circles, and what we had is over."

Brock didn't seem fazed by her words. "I understand that you're upset. I just need you to hear me out."

She shook her head. "I don't need to do anything when it comes to you."

Ian kept his gaze trained on Brock, studying the man. He had met plenty of guys like him at functions and fundraising galas—guys whose image and status climbing were top priority. Brock's forehead was beaded with perspiration, and his hair was slightly damp. Was that coconut Ian smelled? Did the man use essential oils or something?

"Babe," Brock said in a lowered tone. "You can stay mad at me if you want, but I need to tell you about the work I've been doing. I'm a different person now. There's no reason to throw away all that we had together. We can start new, fresh, however you want."

Brandy tilted her head, fire in her eyes. "I'm not mad at you for being confused between two sisters, Brock. It happens. But like I've told you multiple times, I don't need that confusion in *my* life. I truly wish you all the best, but this is the last time I'm going to ask you to stop contacting me. Next time, I'll file harassment charges."

The words seemed to merely bounce off Brock, like he hadn't heard one word of her ultimatum. Then his gaze moved to Ian. "How long have you all been seeing each other? Is this guy the real reason you called things off, Brandy? But you were too chicken to tell me?"

"Ian and I met a few weeks ago. Not that it's any of your business." She stepped toward him, but Brock didn't budge. "What part of *leave me alone* do you not understand?"

Brock's gaze focused on Brandy, his mouth twisted into a smirk. "I understand your confusion, and I don't blame you for being upset with the Everly thing. But this is going too far, Brandy. Dating another guy already?"

"No, *you're* going too far." She took a shaky breath. "Leave, now."

Ian kept his eyes pinned on Brock, waiting for one movement toward Brandy.

The man exhaled slowly, as if he had all the time in the world. Then he put on his sunglasses and walked around to the driver's side of his car. "You're the one who's changed, Brandy. Have a nice life."

He yanked the car door open and slid inside, then

slammed it shut. Seconds later, he pulled out, leaving billowing dust in his wake.

Brandy stared after him, then turned her wide eyes on Ian. "Thanks for not interfering. It would have just given him more fuel."

Ian unclenched his fists. "You might want to report him for trespassing anyway. I don't trust that guy."

Brandy's shoulders sagged. "I can't believe he came here. I didn't think he'd be so brazen—" Her voice cut off, and she covered her mouth, as if she were just realizing all the ramifications of what had just happened.

"Hey," Ian said in a soft voice. He moved to Brandy and pulled her into his arms. He was gratified when she wrapped her arms about his waist and held on.

The afternoon breeze stirred about them, and the silence finally settled once again. Yet the peace had been marred with Brock's visit.

"Come on," Ian said. "Let's go to my place. I want to call Austin and have him pay a visit to Brock."

Brandy drew away and looked up at him. "I don't want this to escalate. Brock got the picture. I think."

"Yeah, you *think*," he said. "I'm not so positive. He can't take rejection, that's for sure. I don't want you to wonder if he'll show up again. Maybe at a time when he knows I'm not around."

Brandy gazed at him for a moment, then nodded. "Okay, but I don't want you or Austin getting into any trouble. Brock's a lawyer."

"Fitting," he mused. "I've dealt with plenty of lawyers, though. He'll know more than anyone that he's crossed the line. Nursing a bruised ego is no excuse for showing up and confronting you."

Duke barked from inside the truck.

"I'll grab a couple of things from the cottage," she said, "then come up to the cabin."

He nodded. "Okay. See you soon." He bent and kissed her cheek, liking that he could do that, and liking that they were finally alone—away from her mother's judgment and from Brock's craziness.

Ian climbed back into the truck. On the short drive to his cabin, he called Austin. When the man picked up the call, Ian said, "Isn't Brock Hayes your cousin or something?"

"Second cousin," Austin said, surprise in his tone. "What's going on?"

"He was waiting for Brandy when we pulled up to her cottage."

"Wait, what? He knows where she lives?"

"Ian?" Everly cut in. "What's going on?"

Ian explained, and she peppered him with more questions. So maybe it was just Everly who needed to know the situation.

"This is crazy," she said. "Austin and I are going to pay him a visit as soon as I get the sheriff."

If Ian hadn't met Brock and seen him in action, he might think this was overboard. "Good. Do you want me to come, too?"

"No," Everly said immediately. "Stay with Brandy. I know she's a tough woman, but that was way over the line. Brock has lost his mind."

Ian hung up after asking Everly and Austin to keep him updated. He parked and got Duke out of the truck. The dog trotted to the tree line, then looked back at him.

"Go ahead, bring Brandy here." Ian headed inside the cabin and quickly straightened up a few things.

Moments later, he heard Brandy's footsteps on the porch. He turned to see her coming in, her eyes wide. "He was inside my cottage."

Everything inside Ian went cold. "What?"

"The door wasn't locked, but I don't think I locked it. Still . . ." She ran a trembling hand over her hair. "I walked inside, and everything felt different. It's hard to explain. So I looked around, and several things had been adjusted, as if he'd picked up stuff and set it back down."

"Okay." Ian grasped her hand and led her to the couch. "Tell me everything you noticed."

So Brandy did, and Ian typed it into his phone. Then he said, "What do you think about filing a report with the sheriff's office?" He explained what he'd talked to Everly and Austin about.

Ian knew Brandy was rattled because she didn't argue with him, not this time.

"All right," she breathed. "I want to talk to my sister first, then we can call the sheriff."

"Of course." He waited while Brandy talked to Everly. Her sister's voice came through loud and clear and angry through the phone.

Then Brandy called the sheriff's office, putting it on speaker.

She answered a bunch of questions, then confirmed that yes, she wanted to press charges for trespassing. At the end of it all, she turned her luminous eyes on Ian. "Do you think I did the right thing?"

"Absolutely." He reached for her, and she moved into his embrace as they leaned against the cushions of the couch.

"Can I ask a favor?" she whispered.

"Anything."

"Can I stay here tonight? On the couch or something? I don't want to be alone."

Ian was really glad Lydia Kane wasn't here to overhear Brandy. And he was glad Brandy felt this comfortable with him. Because he'd just realized that he'd do anything for this woman.

Twenty-Three

BRANDY STARED AT THE CEILING in the dark. Everything was so quiet in Ian's cabin. Well, except the soft snoring of Duke, who'd elected to sleep in the guest room with her. It turned out that she didn't need to sleep on Ian's couch. He had two guest rooms, and one had a bed in it.

After the sheriff's office had taken down all the information about Brock, she'd felt exhausted—three months' worth of exhaustion.

It had taken some convincing, but Everly and Austin had agreed to stay away from Brock.

So it was all over, right?

She exhaled, hoping that was true. Seeing Brock again had rattled her—as she'd suspected it would. He'd looked different, too. Like he spent double the time in the gym. He'd always kept in shape, but now it looked like he obsessed over it, or was maybe taking supplements?

If she could move on, he could move on. She didn't wish terrible things for him—but he needed to learn that no meant no. Turning over on her side, she gazed at the darkened doorway. She'd left the door open—just because—and now she wondered if Ian was still awake. It had to be after midnight.

After a few more minutes of lying awake, she decided to get water from the kitchen. She climbed out of bed and grabbed the sweatshirt Ian had given her. Duke lifted his head from his sleep, his eyes blinking open.

"It's okay, boy," she whispered. "Stay here."

After pulling on the sweatshirt, she walked out of the room. The hallway was dark, of course, but in the kitchen, the moonlight coming through the windows gave plenty of light to move about. She filled a glass with water, then took it out onto the porch. Keeping as silent as possible, she sat on the top step.

An owl hooted somewhere, and Brandy smiled. The low musical tone was somehow soothing. She could very well understand why Ian loved living up here.

His words came back to her from previous conversations of how he regretted getting involved with Ella, and asking himself *what had he been thinking?* Brandy could ask the same questions about herself. Trying to analyze it now probably didn't do her any good, but she could learn from it. Could she trust her attraction to Ian—first that it wasn't a rebound, and that their relationship could be healthy?

A light flickered through the trees, and Brandy straightened, staring at the spot. Maybe it was the reflection of the moon on the leaves, but then she saw it again. Not a flash this time, but more of a sweeping light. Brandy's stomach hollowed. Someone had driven up to her cottage. In the middle of the night.

She rose to her feet, gripping the porch railing. Her

heart hammered, and blood pulsed in her ears. Should she investigate? Calling the cops wouldn't be efficient because she was at least twenty minutes from Everly Falls.

She texted her sister. "Are you at my cottage right now?"

No reply.

"Ian," she whispered. She turned and hurried up the steps, nearly stumbling. Rushing through the cabin, she found his bedroom.

"Ian."

He sat up. "Brandy, what is it?"

"It's... someone's at my cottage. I saw headlights."

Ian was already out of bed, grabbing a shirt. He flipped on the light, and Brandy blinked in the sudden brightness.

"Did you see the car?"

"No, I didn't get any closer."

Ian's face tightened. "Good." He reached for his phone, slipped on his shoes, then moved to his closet. When he pulled out a gun from a small safe on the floor of the closet, Brandy's skin went cold. "Ian..."

"I'm not planning on using it," he said. "But if it's Brock, then he might be armed."

Brandy knew he was right, but it made her feel sick all the same. "Just leave the gun here. It's too risky."

Ian stopped, his green eyes like ice. "Brandy, there's a possible intruder at your house. What do you think would be happening if you were there? I hope it's not Brock, but if it is, we both know he's a loose cannon."

She opened her mouth, then shut it.

"Stay here," he said, then turned to leave. "And keep Duke inside."

"Let's just call the sheriff."

Ian paused again, his jaw working. "Call the sheriff. I'm going to check it out, though."

Brandy stared as he headed down the hall and out the door. Then with trembling fingers, she called the number she'd been on with just hours before. After telling the dispatcher that there was a possible intruder, she headed outside.

No headlights shone through the trees now, and there wasn't any sign of Ian. She couldn't just stand around and wait and wonder. What if she heard gunfire? It would be too late to stop anything. Her stomach felt like it had flipped upside down, but she couldn't just sit at the cabin and wait.

Heart thundering, Brandy hurried down the stairs and approached the path through the trees. She didn't need her phone light—the moon was too bright for that. As she reached the clearing, she paused to catch her breath. Still, there were no sounds anywhere, and the cottage beyond was pitch black. Inching forward, she caught sight of a dark-colored car. Her heart jumped to her throat. Brock had come back. A trespassing citation hadn't even kept him away.

There was no way that his visit to her in the middle of the night was a friendly one. Ian had been right. Brock meant to do her harm—what other explanation could there be?

But where was he now, and where was Ian?

Brandy moved through the trees, away from the car and toward the cottage. She was off the path now, and it was nearly impossible to stay silent, so she had to move very slowly. She froze when she saw movement at the side of the house.

Ian stood there—it had to be him. He was taller and leaner than Brock.

She watched as he peered through a window. Could he see anything? She wanted to tell him to stay out of harm's way. Who knew how Brock would react?

Then, Ian was on the move. He disappeared around the

back of the house. It was then that a flash of light appeared inside the house. Brandy stared at what she knew must be a flashlight. It was too soon for Ian to have climbed in a window, so the only other possibility was that Brock was inside the cottage.

The front door opened silently, and a man stepped out, holding a flashlight. Brock wore all black, including a black baseball cap. Brandy's skin went ice cold. He'd sneaked into her house like a burglar, except he'd assumed she'd be there, too. What was he after? She didn't know if she could allow her brain to go that far.

Yet the evidence was right before her.

Suddenly, the light swung toward the trees, and toward *her*. Brandy held her breath as Brock swept the flashlight back and forth, as if he were looking for something in the trees. Ian's cabin? Surely, Brock hadn't seen her.

She crouched as low as she could, trying not to make a sound. Could he hear her thumping heart, her labored breathing?

Where was Ian now?

What would happen if he and Brock ran into each other? Before she could think up another worry, Brock headed straight for the trees. The light of his flashlight bounced off the trail leading to Ian's cabin.

Brandy released a slow breath as Brock trudged about ten feet from her, up the path to the cabin. It wouldn't take him long to get there. What was he planning on doing? Confronting Ian? Seeing if she was at the cabin, too?

Right now, she was somewhere in between Ian and Brock. Neither of them knew where she was. When she was sure Brock was out of earshot, she pulled out her cell phone. Then she called the dispatcher again.

"Hello, this is Brandy Kane. I have an update on the intruder at my property."

"The sheriff should be at your place in three to four minutes, ma'am. What's the update?"

"The intruder is Brock Hayes, my ex-fiancé. He went into my house and now he's heading to Ian Hudson's cabin. Brock is wearing all black and carrying a flashlight. He might also have a gun."

"Can you verify that, Ms. Kane?"

"No."

She answered a few more questions, then hung up. Minutes . . . that's how long she had to wait for the sheriff. If only she could call him directly. Tell him to continue to Ian's cabin and—

Someone grabbed her around the shoulders, then a hand clamped over her mouth. Brandy tried to twist away, but the man holding her was far stronger. His scent alone gave Brock away—a coconut oil that he mixed with his conditioner.

"Brock," she tried to yell, but it only came out muffled.

"Be quiet," he hissed. "I won't have to hurt you if you cooperate."

Brandy twisted again and tried to scream, but Brock's hold only tightened, crushing her against him.

"Now, where's that boyfriend of yours?" he hissed, tugging her toward the clearing of the cottage. "I know he called the cops on me. Everything between us was fine until he interfered."

Her eyes burned with tears and panic clawed up her throat. She couldn't fall apart now; she had to think. If Brock held her with both hands, that meant he wasn't carrying a gun. Where was his flashlight, though? In his pocket? That could definitely be a weapon, but she wasn't going to let this man drag her around.

She elbowed him as hard as she could in the torso,

which was basically a wall of solid muscle. He grunted. "You want to fight me? You know who'll win, babe."

She whimpered, her tears coming hot and fast now.

"Let her go," a voice growled from somewhere up ahead.

Ian . . . She blinked rapidly to clear her vision, and then she saw him. Standing at the edge of the clearing, a gun pointed directly at her—no, Brock.

"Well, well. Ask and I shall receive," Brock bit out. "Been looking for you."

"Really?" Ian's gun gleamed in the moonlight. "Is that why you broke into Brandy's place, *twice*?"

"Just wanted to see if she was sleeping in her own bed." Brock's voice took on an eerie, singsong tone. "Turns out she's sleeping with *you*—her new man."

Ian took a step forward and demanded once again, "Let her go."

Brock's viselike grip only secured her more tightly against him, his hand now covering her mouth and nose. She tried to gulp in air, but it was futile. It was like breathing through a pillow. If he didn't release her soon, she'd probably pass out.

Maybe she could open her mouth enough to bite his hand? But could she bite hard enough for him to let go?

"Did you know your new boyfriend has a gun?" Brock ground out. "You used to give me crap for that, remember, Brandy? I guess you're two-faced *and* a two-timer. Should have known."

Brandy put all her strength into biting Brock's palm as hard as she could.

"Hey!" he yelped, and then two things happened at once.

Ian fired his pistol, and headlights lit up the clearing.

Brock dropped to the ground, and Brandy twisted out of his relaxed grip.

"You're crazy, man!" Brock screamed.

Had he been hit? Had Ian really just shot the man?

Brandy scrambled away from Brock. He'd pulled his knees to his chest and was covering his head, still yelling. "You're gonna pay for this! I'm a lawyer!"

The clearing flooded with lights from multiple police cars. One of them must have a spotlight.

Brock moved to his knees and lifted his arms. "I'm innocent. That man shot me!"

Brandy huddled behind a tree, blocking her from Brock if he chose to grab her again.

"Drop your weapon," a firm voice commanded.

That was directed toward Ian, Brandy realized. She watched him drop his gun, then raise his arms.

Brock was breathing heavily, but he remained upright and physically fine.

There were four policemen, all advancing across the clearing.

"Hands in the air, ma'am," one of the cops told her.

Brandy obeyed, her entire body trembling. "I'm the one who called in the report," she said. "The man in the clearing is Ian Hudson. He came to check out my place to look for an intruder." She drew in a gulp of air. "The man kneeling is Brock Hayes. He broke into my home tonight, then he . . . assaulted me."

One officer began talking to Ian, as the other three advanced on Brock and handcuffed him.

"I've done nothing," he said. "I just came to talk to my fiancée. That guy over there almost killed me! He's the one who should be arrested."

Brandy's mind blurred as Brock continued to protest,

and one of the cops read him his rights—which only made him more mad.

"Are you all right, ma'am?"

She looked up, into the eyes of the policeman who stood over her.

"I think so," she said above the thundering of her pulse.

"We need to ask you a few questions."

Twenty-Four

IAN COULDN'T BELIEVE WHAT HE was hearing. Well, he could believe it, but it was hard to stomach. It had been two days since the arrest of Brock Hayes, and now Ian sat with Brandy at the sheriff's station while Officer Carlton briefed them on the findings about Brock.

The man was out on bail, but was currently on house arrest.

That didn't make Ian feel particularly happy, but the officer had assured them they were throwing everything in the book at him.

Brandy's hand tightened in his. Ian had been the only one she'd wanted with her. They'd go to her mom's after and talk to the rest of the family about this meeting.

"We found rope, duct tape, alcohol, and firearms in the trunk of Mr. Hayes's car," Officer Carlton said in a grave voice, his brown eyes serious. "We also found a high level of steroids in his blood test. We have every reason to believe that Mr. Hayes's purpose that night was not what he claimed. He went to your place with the intent to harm someone. Either you or Mr. Hudson."

Brandy's face had gone pale, making the bruises about her mouth seem darker. Ian hated that she'd been treated so roughly by Brock, but he also knew it could have been much worse. He'd taken the chance of shooting into the trees above the man, hoping to spook him. It had worked, but having the cops show up at that moment had been a godsend.

"And the assault charges?" Brandy asked in a quiet voice.

"Those will only strengthen the prosecutor's case," Officer Carlton said, gentleness crossing his stoic features.

Brandy had decided to prosecute Brock for his repeated harassment, trespassing, and physical assault. Ian knew it was hard for her to see a man she'd once cared for fall so far, but he was proud of her courage.

Officer Carlton continued with more details and assurances. Then the meeting was over, and they all stood and shook hands.

On the way out of the building, Ian looped his arm about Brandy's shoulders, pulling her close. "Are you all right?"

She leaned into him as they walked. "It's a lot to unpack," she said in an unsteady voice. "I can't believe Brock went off the deep end like that."

"Yeah . . . it's crazy, that's for sure." Ian opened his truck's passenger door for her. He hated to think of what might have happened if Brandy hadn't decided to stay at his place that night. If she'd been alone in that cottage.

They were both quiet as they drove to her mom's house. When they parked in front, Brandy said, "Oh good. My friends aren't here."

She'd told her friends she'd be in touch with them later, after she talked to her family. She didn't want to have a ton of people at her mom's to explain things to.

Walking in, they were greeted by Everly and Austin, too. Everly pulled Brandy into a long hug, then Lydia hugged her daughter. Next, she hugged Ian, surprising him.

"Thank you for watching out for my daughter," she said in a choked voice.

Ian met her watery gaze. "Anytime, Lydia."

She squeezed his hand. "Now, let's hear what the police report said, then we'll eat something. I know you'll all say you're not hungry, but feeding people makes me feel better."

Everyone smiled, but their gazes were still filled with concern. Brandy grasped his hand, and they sat on the love seat together. She began to relay what Officer Carlton had said, but when her voice became too tight to speak, Ian finished the rundown.

Everly's and Lydia's eyes had gone wide, and Austin's face flushed with anger. In fact, at one point, he stood and paced the room at the far end. "I can't believe he's out on bail," he muttered.

"Do you want to stay at my old place above the craft store?" Everly asked Brandy. "The store has a good security system."

"No, she can stay here," Lydia said, her tone insistent. "All the neighbors watch out for each other, and—"

"Mom, I'm not moving home," Brandy said, her voice full strength again. "And thanks, Everly, but I'll be fine. Brock is on house arrest, and we have to trust in our own system. Besides, Ian said I could keep Duke at my place for as long as I want."

She cast him a grateful smile, but he didn't miss the worry still in her eyes. She was putting on a brave face for her family. Would she confide in him? Be open with him? They made it through the motions of Lydia's lunch of chicken croissant sandwiches, fruit salad, and eclairs. Not that Ian was complaining, but Brandy was still pale, and he hoped she'd get the rest she needed.

Once they left her mom's house, Ian felt a burden lift. They now knew Brock's intentions. As rotten as they were, at least they could deal with the facts now. He started up the truck, and they drove out of the neighborhood.

"My guest room is yours for as long as you want it," he said.

Brandy bit her lip. "Are you sure? I mean, the cottage will be totally fine. Duke can be with me, and even though he's a softie, he'll alert me if there's anything."

Ian reached for her hand. "I'm sure."

"I just don't want to be in the way, or uh, you know . . . become too dependent on you."

He slowed at the next light and stopped. Looking over at her, he felt the same pull he'd felt from the first day he'd met her. "I'm here for you, Brandy. Anytime. Whether we are in a relationship or not."

Her gaze locked on to his. "Thank you," she said in a quiet voice. "I don't think I could ever repay you or thank you enough."

"Hey." Ian brought her hand to his mouth and kissed her knuckles. "You helped me out plenty, and I'm not about to let you worry about your safety. No thanks is needed."

"Well, I'll cook you dinners, then."

"I could never turn that down."

Brandy's dimple appeared.

A car behind them honked. He stepped on the gas, then focused on his driving for the next few minutes while his mind whirled. Brandy was going to be staying at his cabin—for who knew how long. He didn't know if that would progress their relationship or not, but he'd leave the ball in her court. Although, he knew that if she tossed the ball his way, he'd be all in.

They drove to her cottage first, and he helped her pack up a few things. Ian didn't miss her nervousness as she opened cupboards and drawers, as if expecting to find some evidence of Brock sorting through her stuff or leaving something behind.

When she had a couple of bags filled with clothing, shoes, and things from the bathroom, she turned to him. "Let's get out the stuff from the fridge, then a few things from the cupboard. I'm assuming you don't have baking essentials."

Ian paused to think.

Brandy smirked. "You have to *think* about it?"

He met her gaze and smiled. "You're right. I have nothing that would be considered baking essentials."

She pulled out a couple of boxes from a closet, and they set to loading them up.

"What's this?" he asked, holding up a plastic jar labeled "Honey Powder."

"Honey powder," she deadpanned.

"For what . . . ?"

"A sugar substitute, but it's also flavorful."

"Ah." Ian turned the jar so he could see the label. "There's honey and sugar in the ingredients list. Kind of defeats the purpose of using it as a sugar substitute."

Brandy laughed. "Just put it in the box, Mr. Hudson."

He obeyed with a chuckle.

When they unloaded everything at his cabin, Duke was waiting for them.

"Hey, buddy." Brandy stopped to pet the dog. "Wanna be roommates for a while?"

"Just because you're taking over the guest bedroom doesn't mean you have to take over my dog, too."

Brandy's blue eyes focused on him. "I'm taking over your kitchen, too. Don't forget that."

Ian exaggerated a sigh.

Brandy was smiling again. That was all he wanted to see.

Inside the cabin, she made a big show of filling the refrigerator and cupboards with "proper food," then setting up her laptop at the kitchen table. "This way I can keep an eye on your workshop," she said in a light voice.

But he wasn't fooled. She wanted to be able to see if anyone was approaching the cabin.

Duke sniffed every item that they unpacked, then followed them to the guest bedroom, where Brandy began to fill the closet with her stuff. "I think you have a new best friend," Ian mused.

She merely smiled and continued arranging her shoes.

"Need help unpacking this?" he asked, moving the final bag onto the bed.

She turned from the closet, and Ian frowned. Her eyes were filling with tears.

"Hey, you're okay." He reached her in two steps and pulled her into his arms.

Her shuddering breath vibrated against his chest. "I think it's finally sinking in."

He nodded and rubbed a hand over her back. They stood for several moments like that inside the walk-in closet, holding each other. Finally, Brandy drew in a deep breath. "I'll be okay. Thanks for the hug."

He drew away then, but didn't let her go. "I'm glad you're here," he murmured. "And I hope you feel safe."

"I do." She lifted up on her feet and pressed a kiss on his mouth.

Ian could definitely get used to this. He kissed her back

gently, knowing that she was in a fragile state of mind. Brandy's body melted against his, warm and soft, and he deepened the kiss. But he kept his hands at her hips. Now that they'd be living in the same space, he'd need to not give in to the temptations that swirled in his head.

"You're one tempting woman," he whispered against her mouth before drawing away.

Brandy's blue eyes had deepened to twilight. "You make it sound like a bad thing."

"Not a bad thing at all." He moved his hand to run his fingers along her jaw, above the bruising. "I don't want to take advantage of you or this situation."

The edge of Brandy's mouth lifted. "Living together is going to complicate things."

"Yeah . . ." Ian kissed the edge of her mouth. "I don't mind complicated, though."

Somewhere in the cabin, one of their phones rang. "Yours or mine?" she asked.

"I don't know. Maybe one of us needs to change our ringtone."

Brandy smiled, then stepped out of his arms. For now, the tears were gone. She headed out of the bedroom, Duke trotting after her.

"It's mine," she called out. Then her murmured voice followed.

Ian scrubbed a hand through his hair and took a moment to stand in the room by himself. These were good changes. He wasn't celebrating the circumstances that had led to this situation, but he'd embrace it now that it had happened.

When he walked out of the bedroom, it sounded like Brandy was talking to her sister on the phone. He continued down the hallway, then paused before entering the kitchen.

Brandy sat perched on one of the kitchen chairs, her chin resting on her propped hand, Duke at her feet as if he sat there every day.

Ian was struck by how natural she looked in his cabin, and how comfortable he was having her here. He'd lived alone for so long, and before that, his relationship with Ella was like living in a house made of eggshells. He never thought he'd feel so comfortable *not* being alone.

Brandy caught sight of him and motioned for him to come into the kitchen, just as she said, "I'm not alone in the cottage, Everly." Her gaze focused on Ian and she smiled. "I'm staying at Ian's. I just didn't want to bring it up in front of Mom. You know how she'd be—warning me about running into another man's arms."

Brandy paused, then continued. "Well, maybe I am, but these are arms that I like."

Ian's brows shot up, and he leaned against the counter.

"Okay," she said. "I'll see you at the fall festival." Another pause. "I don't know, I haven't asked him."

Asked him what?

Brandy laughed. "Bye, Everly."

When she hung up, Ian raised his brows.

"Well . . ." she hedged, then stood from the table. She walked toward him, stopping about a foot away. "The fall festival is a tradition in our family. And I wondered if you'd want to go with me. It would kind of be a big deal, though."

He gazed into her porcelain-blue eyes. "Why?"

"Because." She placed her hands on his biceps, then moved them upward, stopping at his shoulders. "People will see us together and assume we're boyfriend and girlfriend. You know how small-town gossip is. And I'd have to introduce you to a lot of people because they'd want to meet you. Which would mean you can't be the reclusive and mysterious man in the cabin anymore."

"Boyfriend-girlfriend, huh?" Ian murmured. "Is that what you want?"

"We are living together," she said, equally softly. "I mean, not for conventional reasons, but I do really like you. And I think you like me?"

She didn't even need to ask that question.

"I do."

Brandy lifted her chin. "Enough to go public at the fall festival?"

"Is that like Facebook official?" he teased.

"Even worse—or better, depending on how you view it."

Ian slipped his hands about her waist and pulled her flush against him. He loved how Brandy's cheeks colored. "I'd love to be your date at the fall festival, Miss Kane."

Twenty-Five

BRANDY WATCHED AS IAN WALKED around the front of the truck to open the passenger-side door for her. Beyond the parking lot, the fall festival was in full swing. She should be more excited to be here, but truthfully, her pulse was jumping.

Spending time again in Everly Falls would take some getting used to, even though Brock had shattered her peace at the cottage. There were so many things in town that reminded her of being with him. Choosing their wedding cake at the bakery, meeting for coffee at Marshall's, walks in the park . . . then fast-forward to the night in the park where she'd taken refuge after finding out the truth.

Everly had found her there, and that's when Brandy decided to call things off permanently.

The truck door opened, and there stood Ian, dressed in dark jeans and a sage-colored shirt that made his eyes deep green. He hadn't shaved in a couple of days, and the dark scruff along his jaw made him even more handsome. When Ian extended his hand, she took a deep breath, then grasped it.

This was it. Her reentry into Every Falls. It had been months since she'd seen most of these people, and there were bound to be questions. She wouldn't let the questions bother her, though. Not with Ian at her side.

Perhaps she'd become too dependent on him, but right now, she needed his steady presence.

"You okay?" he asked in a low voice after he closed the truck door.

"Yeah." Was her voice too high-pitched? "Just don't leave me."

Ian squeezed her hand. "I'm not planning on it."

Brandy nodded, even though she knew he'd stick by her side. It was what they did. Stuck together. She'd finally told her mom she was staying at Ian's cabin. She knew her mom disapproved, but she'd mercifully kept her opinions to herself.

"There you are," Steph said, striding toward them. She held the hand of the man who was her flavor of the week. "This is Cliff." She released him and hugged Brandy. "You came—I'm so glad. Are you freaking out?"

Brandy smiled. "I'm fine." She wasn't about to discuss anything about Brock right now.

Cliff was a couple of inches shorter than Steph, but his Hawaiian shirt exuded confidence. "Nice to meet you both." He shook Ian's hand, then Brandy's. "Want to join us at one of the food trucks?"

"We have to go find my mom first," Brandy said.

"Oh, she's ordering everyone around." Steph laughed, her gaze taking in Ian, then looking over at Brandy with a wink. "Have fun, you two."

They spent the next hour greeting friends or acquaintances, with Brandy introducing Ian over and over. He had no problem talking to people, and she caught a glimpse of his business acumen. When they reached the booth ran by Gentry Martin, who worked for the mayor in accounting, the woman appraised Ian before saying, "You're the one who saved Brandy from Brock?"

"I wouldn't exactly say 'saved.'"

Gentry waved a hand, her multiple silver rings catching the sunlight. She wore enough makeup to be ready for a photo shoot should one arise. "Tomatoes, to-mah-toes. She's in good hands, according to Lydia—that's all that matters."

"Agreed," Ian said, amusement in his tone.

"Well, then," Gentry continued, looking him up and down again. "Let's put you to good use. Can you move these boxes under the tables?"

So Ian set to work, and Brandy helped Gentry arrange the Christmas stockings she'd knitted. Brandy didn't know how she worked a full-time job and knitted so much throughout the year. She had given Brandy college advice, since she was an accountant.

Customers came and went. Most of them were talked into a purchase by Gentry.

Ian stood by, like he'd promised, and participated when asked.

"What's this?" someone said, and Brandy looked over to see Lori and Julie, who carried her one-year-old on her hip.

"Hi," Brandy said with a smile, and walked out of the booth to hug her friends.

"He came?" Lori whispered conspiratorially.

"He did," Brandy whispered back.

"I can see why you've become the recluse in the hills," Julie said. "If I weren't married, I'd be living at the cottage, too."

Brandy laughed. "Whatever. Come say hi." She quite enjoyed the attention her friends gave Ian and his patient answers. His eyes twinkled with amusement, so she knew he wasn't too bugged.

Twenty-Six

IAN LIKED THE WAY BRANDY'S hand fit in his, and how her fingers clasped his, warm and sure. Not to mention she wasn't making it a secret that they were together. In front of all her friends. It also meant he felt impatient to have her all to himself again. He was barely following the chatter between the women.

Yet, once Brandy's friends left, Jessica found them, her hair in pigtails. Everly and Austin weren't far behind. "Did you bring Duke?"

"I should have brought him," Ian said with a chuckle. "He would have loved to play with you."

Jessica beamed. "Maybe you can bring him to my house." She turned to Austin. "Dad, can we invite Ian and Brandy to our house so I can play with Duke?"

"Uh, sure." Austin looked at them, laughter in his eyes.

"Yeah, let's do that," Everly agreed. "Do you guys want to come for dinner tomorrow night?"

Brandy glanced over at Ian, and he could see the question in her eyes—was this too much all at once?

"I think Duke would love that," he said.

"Yay!" Jessica squealed and wrapped her arms about Ian's legs.

When it was determined that Everly and Austin would take a turn helping at the booth, which Jessica was thrilled about, Ian walked with Brandy toward the line of food trucks.

"Are you sure it's okay to go to Austin's for dinner?" she asked him.

He looked over at her. "Yeah, I'm sure."

She pulled him to a stop. They'd reached a place in the shade under a sprawling tree. "I know this is a lot. I don't want my family running over you like a freight train."

He knew she was being sincere, but he also knew she hoped he'd refute her statement. And he wanted to, because he was happy to spend all the time he could with her, and that meant her family's events. "If I think about Duke, he'll be more than happy to go. And if I think about you, you'll enjoy the time with your sister. And if I think about me, well, I just want to be where you are."

Brandy's eyes brightened and the pink returned to her cheeks. "Why are you so easy to persuade?"

"I'm a weak man around you," he said with a laugh.

"Hmm."

Her dimple appeared, so he leaned down and kissed it.

"PDA?" she whispered, slipping her arms around his waist.

"I don't mind if you don't."

"I don't mind."

So he kissed her on the mouth. He kept it brief, but he didn't let her go. She smiled up at him, then she turned her head, her attention caught by something.

When Ian saw the color drain from her cheeks, he

looked over. At first, he only saw people walking around, kids playing in a bounce house, and a line that had formed at a food truck. Then he saw the figure standing on the far side of the park, by a small brick building that must be the restrooms.

Even though they were pretty far away, the hair on the back of Ian's neck stood up. "Go back to the booth with your sister," he said in a low voice. "Call the police."

"Ian, don't..."

But he stepped away and began striding toward Brock. The man was violating his house arrest if he was hanging out at the park. Ian pulled out his phone and started to film. There was no doubt it was Brock, although he wore a dark sweatshirt and dark ball cap pulled low over his eyes.

Ian had taken about a dozen steps by the time Brock saw him and clued in to the fact that he was being filmed. Brock turned and strode away, checking over his shoulder more than once. Ian continued following.

When Brock reached the parking lot on the far side, he began to run. Ian ran, too, still filming.

Only when Brock disappeared across the street and turned down a side road did Ian slow his pace. Two cop cars were pulling around the parking lot, and Ian filled them in on Brock's direction.

It didn't take long.

Ian waited in the parking lot until Officer Carlton circled back around to talk to him.

"Brock ran into the corner bookshop," the officer said through the open window of his patrol car. "Must have panicked. He's being taken into custody now."

"Where's his probation officer?"

Officer Carlton had the decency to redden. "He was at

the festival. He's a newer hire and wasn't paying close attention to his job of tracking."

Ian gave a short nod. "Is Brock going to get a slap on his hand again?"

Carlton's jaw worked. "We're transferring him to the state prison to await his court hearing. He's used up his nine lives here."

"That's good to know." Ian was relieved, but Brock should have never made it as far as the park. "Can you let me know when Brock is in fact out of Everly Falls?"

"I will."

Ian stepped away from the patrol car. He didn't know where Brandy was, but he needed to find her and give her the update. He called her number and she answered on the first ring.

"Where are you?" he asked.

"At your truck." Her voice was breathless. "What happened?"

"They arrested him again." Ian strode in the direction of the truck. "I'll fill you in when I get there."

A few minutes later, Ian spotted Brandy sitting on the curb next to his truck with Everly and Austin. When she spotted him, she rose to her feet and began walking toward him, leaving the others behind. Seeing the worry on her pale face made him sick all over again. When would Brock be out of their lives for good?

Brandy didn't say anything at first, just stepped into his arms.

He pulled her close and kissed the top of her head.

"Why did you chase after him?" she finally asked. "He could have been armed."

"That would have been a feat since all of his weapons

were confiscated." Ian drew away and brushed his hands down her arms. "They're taking him out of Everly Falls to await his court hearing. I guess Officer Carlton is finally cracking down."

Relief crossed Brandy's features. "Oh good."

"When's his court hearing?" Austin asked. He and Everly had reached them.

"Next week," Brandy said, turning to face them.

"We'll be there," Austin said.

Everly looked surprised at her fiancé's statement, but she only nodded.

"Oh, and I found out that Brock was fired from his job," Austin continued. "Talked to my dad's cousin and learned that Brock's family has totally disowned him, too."

"Wow, I guess the Kane sisters really did him in," Everly mused.

"I think his problems go back a lot further," Ian said. "You ladies just got the worst of it."

Everly nodded. "You're probably right, but I'll leave that for the prison psychologist to figure out."

Ian reached for Brandy's hand. "If you want to leave, I can take you."

"Yeah, I can let Mom know," Everly offered.

Brandy looked at Ian, her eyes less panicked now, but there was still worry there. Then she faced her sister. "I'm staying. I've let Brock keep me away from things I used to love. But I'll just need a minute, okay?"

"Of course." Everly stepped forward and hugged her tightly. "We'll be at Gentry's booth."

As Everly and Austin walked away, Brandy turned to Ian. "Can we sit in the truck for a little bit? I just need to process everything."

"Yeah, sure." They climbed into his truck, and Brandy

nestled against him, wrapping her arms about his waist.

She closed her eyes, and he almost thought she'd fallen asleep, when she spoke. "I'm going to move back into my cottage. Brock is in jail now, and probably won't be getting out anytime soon."

"True . . ." Ian felt his stomach flip, but was it because he was still worried about her safety or just liked her living under his roof? "There's no rush. I mean, I could cook more if it will convince you to stay longer."

Brandy lifted her head. "I don't need convincing, Ian," she said in a slow voice. "I'd love to stay, but I also need to prove to myself that I can conquer my fear over what almost happened with Brock. I can't live life on *almosts* and *maybes*. The anxiety alone will just cripple me."

Ian kissed her temple, then pulled her fully into his arms. "You're an amazing woman, Brandy. If you need to do this, then I'll try not to take it personally."

He could feel her smile against his neck, and that was all that he cared about—her well-being and happiness. His world had gone from an implosion to very, very small, to now expanding and coming to life again. And he loved it.

Twenty-Seven

CONGRATULATIONS, STEPH TEXTED. *YOU'RE OFFICIALLY the Bad-A of our group.*

I'll own it, Brandy wrote back to the group text.

You'd better! Lori replied. *It's not every day that one of us takes down a perp in court and gets him consecutive sentences.*

Well, that was the lawyer, Brandy wrote.

True, Julie added. *Maybe we should invite him to our party.*

Is he single? Steph asked.

Brandy sent a laughing emoji, then wrote, *No lawyers at my party. See you guys soon. I'm signing off. There's a man I need to see about.*

Oooo, Lori wrote.

Julie sent a row of heart emojis.

You owe us a very detailed update, Steph texted.

Brandy didn't even reply. She'd been home from the court hearing for about an hour. Ian had gone with her, of course, and then dropped her off at her cottage when she'd insisted she'd be fine alone. She'd known he didn't want to leave, but in truth, she needed a bit of space from him as well.

Plugging her phone into the charger, she went outside and sat on the old rocking chair she kept on the porch. In an hour, the clearing would be filled with her family and friends. They were having a barbecue to celebrate Brock's incarceration. Kind of strange to think about celebrating something like that. But maybe Brandy had more of her mom in her than she'd thought. Good food and company would help them all cope and move on.

Brock had been sentenced on more than one count, each of them carrying five-year prison terms, which would be served consecutively. It was surreal to think that this was all over—totally and one hundred percent. Seeing Brock Hayes in one of his lawyer suits at the courthouse, facing criminal charges, was like karma hitting him square in the nose.

Good riddance, was all Brandy could think as she watched him led out of the courtroom, handcuffed and ankle chained.

Then she'd cried. Everly and her mom had hugged her. Austin had hugged her. Officer Carlton had hugged her. And Ian had hugged her. She'd been surrounded by love and support and friendship, while Brock was led away to live out the next years surrounded by cement walls and iron bars.

Brandy tucked her feet under her as she leaned back in the rocking chair. The trees rattled in the soft wind and the scent of crisp fall air swirled around her. As much as she loved her friends and family, she'd grown used to the peace and quiet in the hills. She'd also grown used to the man and his dog just a few hundred steps away. And she'd grown used to waking up to sounds of nature and falling asleep to the call of the owl.

Her gaze strayed in the direction of Ian's cabin.

Over the past couple of days, Brandy had realized two things. First, that Ian had come into her life at the most perfect moment, and she'd jumped in perhaps too eagerly. Although she couldn't blame herself. She couldn't think of any other man, or person for that matter, who she'd want at her side during the most hellacious moments of her adult life.

The second thing she'd realized was that she was in love with him.

And this time, it was the real deal.

She was pretty sure he loved her back, but neither of them had said anything. What would change if she admitted it? She knew she'd feel like she was being more authentic with him. And even if he didn't say the words back, or feel the same way, she wanted him to know. He deserved to know. After all he'd been through, and heck, after all she'd been through, Ian needed to know that he was the most important person in her life.

So . . . she was going to tell him. Right now. Before her yard and cottage filled with people. And whatever happened, happened.

Brandy stood from the chair and headed across the clearing. The path leading to Ian's cabin was well-worn now with their many trips back and forth. The air was cooling fast, and Brandy wondered if she should turn back and grab a sweatshirt. But she was more than halfway to the cabin by now.

Once she cleared the trees, she heard the sound of hammering start up from Ian's workshop. Was he not getting ready for the party? But then again, what did he really need to do to get ready? They'd bought a bunch of food together the day before in town, and Ian said he'd man the grill.

Brandy headed toward the workshop. The door was partly open, and Duke came out just as she reached it.

"Hey, buddy." She bent to pet his soft head and silky ears. "Are you coming to the party, too?"

The hammering had stopped, of course, and Brandy felt Ian's assessing gaze on her. Probably wondering if there was a specific reason she was at his workshop when guests would be arriving soon.

"Everything okay?" he asked in that deep voice of his.

She wondered how many times he'd asked her that since they'd first met. Lifting her gaze, she found his green eyes studying her. His forearms were dusted with sawdust, and his shaven face had a light sheen of perspiration.

"Everything's okay," she said, and it was.

At Ian's smile, her heart swelled.

"Need my help?" he asked.

"Always."

He chuckled and pulled off his work gloves. "I guess I can take a break," he teased.

Brandy walked toward him, running her fingers along a finished bookcase, then she stopped in front of the cabinet he'd been hammering. "This a new order?"

"It goes with the bookcase," he said. "The customer just added it."

"Ah, smart customer," she teased.

"It's Pete, actually."

She looked up at him, gazing into the eyes that she'd come to trust, that she loved so much. "Pete? Really?"

"Yeah . . . he's been reaching out more and more, and we have sort of a truce. No talking about the woman who came between us." Ian shrugged. "Maybe there's a future for a renewed friendship. Time will tell." His brows dipped. "How are you feeling?"

"Really great."

Something like relief crossed his features. "I'm glad. I was worried about dropping you off."

She closed the distance between them and looped her arms about his neck. Ian didn't hesitate in the least and pulled her close, his hands moving behind her back.

"What's this for?" he murmured, his gaze locked with hers.

"Just because." Then she kissed him. He was a little overheated, and smelled of wood shavings, but she didn't mind.

Ian's mouth was warm as he kissed her back, and Brandy let herself become lost in him for a few moments. It was easy to do, and besides, they were celebrating. Ian lifted her onto the work table, and she wrapped her legs around his waist as his kissing deepened.

Brandy sighed into him, letting all her senses get tangled in everything that was him—his scent, his warmth, his strong arms, his beating heart, his breath against her neck as his kissing traveled lower.

"Ian," she said at last. "I need to tell you something."

Slowly, he lifted his head, and she waited until the fog cleared from his eyes.

"Is it something good?" he rasped.

"That depends."

His expression changed. "On what?"

"On you." She drew in a breath, her fingers stroking the edge of his collar. "I wanted to tell you something . . . before everyone arrives and the chaos descends."

He nodded, but his body had tensed.

"It's pretty simple, actually," she said in a quiet voice.

"But very important."

"Brandy . . . you're killing me."

She flashed a smile. "Okay, here it is. I'm in love with you. I know it's hard to believe since we haven't been neighbors for long, and I've been a total mess through it all, but—"

Ian cradled her face with his hands and kissed her.

Brandy clung to his arms, kissing him back. This must be a good sign, right?

After a long moment, Ian broke off their kiss. He was smiling. "You're not a mess, Brandy. And if you think you are, then you're a beautiful mess—one that *I* love."

She stared at him, and his eyes crinkled as he continued. "I love you more than I ever thought my cold heart could ever love another person."

Brandy half laughed, half cried. "And how much is that?"

Ian's fingers moved along her jaw, then behind her neck. He rested his forehead against hers. "More than the stars hanging over Everly Falls."

"That's a lot of stars."

"Yes." His mouth found hers again, and she tightened her hold around his neck, slipping her fingers into his hair.

When she had to catch her breath, she drew away. "I'm really glad you love me back, or this would have been awkward."

Ian chuckled and ran his hands across her shoulders and down her back. "We could survive awkward."

Duke barked in agreement, heading out of the workshop.

"I think he hears people," Ian said, still holding her close.

"Is it time already?" she murmured.

"Probably." He kissed her briefly again, then helped her off the table. "I'm glad you came into my workshop for your serious talk."

She smirked as she threaded their fingers. "I didn't scare you off?"

"No, the opposite." He walked with her outside, where Duke was waiting by the tree line, tail thumping. "You're not going to get rid of me now, Ms. Kane."

"I won't complain."

Ian tugged her to a stop and gazed down at her, his eyes matching the dark pines around them. "Good. Because I'm not going anywhere."

"Me neither," she whispered, her heart pounding. Voices could be heard coming from the direction of the cottage—people had definitely arrived.

His mouth curved. "Does your mom know about your decision?"

"She will soon enough." Brandy set a hand on his chest. "My heart's here, and I love everything about this place."

"Me too." Ian's hand covered hers. "What do you think about making this place a . . . permanent home?"

Brandy's heart rate zoomed upward. "Permanent as in you and me . . . living here?"

"A little more than that." He moved his other hand to her shoulder, his fingers skimming her neck. "I know it's too soon, but you're the only woman I see in my future. So . . . when the time's right, maybe I can talk you into marrying me."

She wasn't sure she'd heard him right, but he was standing right in front of her, saying those words.

"I'll wait as long as you want," he said softly. "As long as you need."

Her throat went tight, and her eyes burned. "Ian . . ."

His fingers moved behind her neck, his touch gentle and warm. "Don't worry, I'm not asking for any answers right now. When you're ready."

She drew in a shaky breath, and then she threw her arms about his neck and hugged him fiercely.

"I guess that's a future yes?" he asked with a chuckle.

"I love you," she whispered.

"I love you, too," he whispered back.

Duke gave another eager bark. The voices and commotion had increased at the cottage.

"I guess we'd better go join the party," she whispered against his neck.

"Hmm. Okay."

Reluctantly, she released Ian, and they set off along the path, hand in hand. Brandy's heart was so full, she wondered if it would burst. As the autumn leaves crunched beneath their shoes, she wondered how many more times she'd walk through these trees until she was ready to make things with Ian permanent.

Not long, her heart whispered. *Not long at all.*

Want to read Everly & Austin's story in *Just Add Romance*?

Continue reading for a Sneak Peek:

One

IT WASN'T THAT EVERLY KANE didn't want a man in her life, it was more like she hadn't found one without a major flaw. And by major, she meant someone who was still in love with his ex-wife, or still lived with his parents, or insisted on being called by his gaming name, Pete-87.

Unfortunately, Everly had dated each of those type of men at least once. The guy in love with his ex? Twice. Different guys, same major flaw.

And . . . this made it easier for Everly not to feel guilty when inventing a budding relationship on the phone with her mother. Especially when her younger sister's wedding was in three weeks.

"Honey," her mother murmured into the phone. "Are you sure you're okay? You sound upset."

"I'm fine, Mom," Everly said. "Really. I'm exhausted from work and class." Truthfully, she hadn't wanted to answer her mom's phone call because she'd just pulled up to the Everly Falls movie theater. It was a Wednesday night, and very few people would be at the movies, exactly how Everly liked it.

Oh, and that's right, Everly was named after her own town. It was a joke that got very old, very fast, in grade school. She pushed the thought away.

The movie started in ten minutes, and unlike the rest of the general population in America, she loved the previews. She'd analyze each one, then mark in her Notes app whether the upcoming movies were a must-see, see-only-if-nothing-else-good-is-playing, or a hard-pass.

Everly also needed about eight minutes to buy a ticket, get popcorn and soda, then be in her seat before the lights dimmed. It was part of the transition from real world to movie world. It gave her goosebumps every time.

"All right, honey," her mom continued, in a sympathetic tone that had gotten on Everly's nerves lately. "We'll see you tomorrow at the bridal shower, all right? And you can tell us all about this mystery man you're dating. Tom, is it? What's his last name?"

"Uh, Middleston." Everly winced. Had she channeled the actor she was about to watch in one of the Avengers movies? Their town theater had two auditoriums—one showed new releases, the other showed oldies, but goodies.

"Wonderful, dear," her mother said. "We'll look forward to hearing all about Tom Middleston tomorrow."

Everly's voice was very, very small when she said, "Okay, bye Mom." She hung up, the small pit in her stomach feeling like it had grown to a full-sized apple now.

Was it so horrible to pretend that she was dating someone? She'd had pretend boyfriends before—guys she'd talked about when she was in middle school and high school—when the popular girls were throwing around words like *dating, kissing, holding hands* . . . Once Everly had declared she had a boyfriend, who lived in her cousin's town, so she only got to see him on family visits, and suddenly, Everly wasn't the frumpy girl in school with the wild, curly hair. She was the interesting girl.

Everly sighed and climbed out of her car. The wind was warm for June, and it stirred her messy bun, making it even messier.

A pretend boyfriend was probably fine when she was a teenager. But now? At twenty-seven? Perhaps not so fine.

But desperate times called for desperate measures, right?

As in when your gorgeous little sister, Brandy, was getting married in a few weeks to the equally gorgeous Brock Hayes. Who was pretty much amazing in every way, expect for one tiny detail. One tiny, but significant detail.

He was Everly's ex-boyfriend.

She pushed down the bitterness that she'd kept firmly buried and tucked her jacket under her arm as she crossed the nearly empty parking lot. It might be a warm June night, but she always brought a jacket for the theater. She adjusted her messy bun, which she'd once had decent before work that day. She thought her job at the craft store was fun, but her mother didn't think so and considered it an aimless career.

But Everly loved the organized aisles of craft items and the potential in each item to create something unique. It combated the topsy-turvy world of expectations outside the craft shop. Even in her sleepy town, it seemed that everyone was living a full, accomplished life. Her girlfriends from high school were either in great careers or getting married. Or married with a kid. Or . . .

Everly pulled open the theater door as her cell phone buzzed with a text.

OMG, Mom told me you're dating someone! I want to hear all about it!

The text, alas, was from Brandy. There was no way Everly could carry on this fib any longer. Her mom might believe her, but Brandy would see through it in an instant. Everly sighed, and without opening the text—so her sister wouldn't know she'd read it—she turned off her phone. Another rule she had about going to the movies. No phones. No distractions.

She bought her ticket at the snack counter.

"Hi, Everly," Janlyn said. She was a teenager who worked at the snack counter, her dark, soulful eyes rarely smiled.

Which is why Everly made sure to greet her cheerfully. "Great to see you, Jan. How's everything going?"

"Oh, you know, the same."

It was the same—the same response she always gave.

"Oh, okay," Everly said. "Ticket for one, please. I'm seeing the Avengers."

"The usual snacks?"

Which was a medium popcorn and medium Dr. Pepper. Yep. Everly had a standing order at the movie theater. She nodded sheepishly and tapped on the counter while she waited.

Jan returned a moment later with both snacks.

Everly picked everything up and headed toward the theater room. Her hands were full, so she used her shoulder to push through the door. She'd been right. Only a handful of other people were inside. She picked her favorite spot—

middle aisle, middle seat. The only way to get the full effect of course.

She briefly toyed with the thought of turning on her phone and answering her sister, but then a string of texts would follow. The lights would be dimming any minute, and Everly didn't want the distraction. Besides, she still hadn't made up the story of how she'd met Tom—ahem, Middleston—or what he looked like, etc.

Just as the lights lowered, a tall man walked into the theater. Alone. A quick glance told Everly that he was one of those confident, good-looking types. He had brownish hair that was long enough to touch his collar, deep-set eyes, broad shoulders, and he was built yet lean. He probably had a girlfriend or wife joining him any minute. Which meant that Everly should not be checking him out. But she'd never seen him before, and she knew everyone in town.

Was he passing through town? Here on a work trip? Visiting his in-laws?

His clothing was generic for the most part—jeans that fit him quite nicely, and a gray or blue t-shirt beneath a darker colored jacket.

The theater went dark then, illuminated only by the screen showing a commercial reminding everyone to silence their phones and be respectful of their neighbors.

The tall man hadn't found a seat yet, but remained near the entrance, as if he were scanning the chairs.

Maybe he was picky like her? Everly's gaze shifted back to the screen as a movie trailer started, it was some thriller with a bunch of teenagers in it. She dug her small notebook out of her bag and jotted down the title of the movie, ranking it a three—middle of the road.

The man was still standing by the entrance, scanning seats.

Sit down already, Everly wanted to say. The second trailer started, one of those high-action car chase movies. She wrote down the title, then ranked it a one—a must-see.

The man started forward, and soon he climbed the steps, getting closer to her middle row. She fully expected him to continue on past her row, but he didn't. He turned right into her row.

Everly didn't move. Couldn't. There were literally dozens of empty rows.

Yet, the man with the broad shoulders and well-fitted jeans continued down *her* row, getting closer and closer to her. Until he stopped.

Everly's breathing stopped with him. No, she didn't turn her head, but she could very well see him in her peripheral vision. She knew exactly how many seats away he sat from her when he sat down.

Two.

Two

AUSTIN HAYES HAD WANTED TO turn down this job. Renovating an old theater in a small town closer to his home would have been fine. But not in Everly Falls. The theater itself was charming, although severely outdated. From the moment he walked into the building he could smell the decades-old popcorn grease, but beyond that, he was already calculating the amount of work that would need to be done.

Tomorrow, he'd get a copy of the blueprints from Town Hall, and that's when the real calculations would begin.

Tonight, he was coming to the theater as a regular moviegoer. To check things out from a distance and to gauge his first impressions.

His dad had apparently visited relatives in Everly Falls as a kid, and he was the type to keep in touch with friends over the years. So, the city council had contacted his dad about the job. According to him, there was something sentimental about the place. The problem was, his dad's hip surgery had put him out of commission for a couple of months, and possibly for much longer. So here Austin was instead of his dad. A hundred miles away from home on a two-to-three-month job. Which meant that there would be few chances to see his seven-year-old daughter, Jessica. Thankfully, his mom had stepped in to help with Jessica.

Being away from Jessica so much hadn't been the path he wanted. Of course, that had been the pattern of his life the past few years. When his wife had died from cancer a couple of years ago, that had definitely not been the path he'd chosen. Becoming a single dad with a young daughter had not been his plan. Neither had the long and lonely months that had followed when his mother's friends, and his mother herself, had tried to set him up with one woman or another.

Everyone had given him space for about six months, then the interference set in.

"Jessica needs a mother," Austin's mom had said with more and more frequency. "We all miss Rachel, but it's okay to move on. She would have wanted that for you."

But Austin rarely had free time, and when he did, Jessica was his priority. Still, he had been on a handful of token dates, and honestly, none of them had struck him as mother material for Jess. He'd even kissed one of the women, and she'd then wanted to move past all of the relationship steps and move in together.

No thanks.

Once Austin was settled into his seat at the theater, he tried to forget everything for a few hours. A woman sat a couple of seats over in the seat he would normally have preferred. Middle of the middle was always the best seat in a theater. Rachel used to tease him about it.

Memories like that made him miss her. During the early days of their marriage, that was. Times like this, when it was just him, and he wasn't focused on work, the good memories flooded back. Despite the opening action scenes of the most recent Avengers movie, Austin was barely paying attention. Although the not-so-good memories were more recent, when he thought of Rachel, he tried to think only of their early marriage together.

They had always been in sync. Loved the same foods, the same recreation, the same type of decorating for their house . . . Eventually, though, their lives had become routine, predictable, even *boring*. Just as Rachel had accused him of being.

She wanted a baby as much as he did, and when Jessica was born, they both doted on her. The first couple of years, anyway. Then Rachel went back to work at a salon, and things slowly shifted in their relationship. She had started spending more and more time after work with her coworkers. They'd meet for dinners and girls-only weekend events.

Austin didn't mind at first, until the day Rachel announced that she was going to start staying over a few nights a week at Taylor's so that she didn't have to deal with the hairy commute. Austin was dead set against it because Jessica needed her mom and her dad.

But Rachel wouldn't budge. Then four months later, she was diagnosed with cancer.

One week after the funeral, a man named Taylor called Austin, asking him to come and fetch Rachel's things. It turned out that the woman Taylor, was really a *man* named Taylor.

"Excuse me, sir?" someone said above him.

It took Austin a moment to realize he had fallen asleep in the movie theater, and the movie was now over. He blinked open his eyes to see a woman standing above him. He guessed her to be the same woman from his row.

Had he been dreaming about Rachel? He hadn't even realized he'd fallen asleep. Yeah, he was tired, but still, *Avengers* should have kept him conscious.

"Sir? Do you speak English?"

"Uh, yeah." His voice was raspy from his impromptu nap.

The woman gazed at him, her head tilted and hazel eyes curious. Her dark blonde hair was a riot of curls and braids with metal things on them, pulled up into a messy bun. And her clothing . . . he wasn't sure he'd ever seen so many different colors on a single person before. Her top was dark pink, and her jacket was some sort of yellow. Her red jeans followed her curves like they'd been painted on.

"The theater has cleared out," she said, her tone low and mellow.

Austin nodded, although his head still felt heavy from sleep. "Thanks, I guess I fell asleep." The screen was completely dark as if the credits had finished rolling too.

Instead of moving on, like most people might—most strangers that was—the woman said, "Long day?"

"You could say that." Austin rose to his feet and stifled a yawn.

The woman still hadn't left.

She was several inches shorter than him, yet he guessed that her personality was far from small. She carried a shoulder bag that looked more like a folded quilt, and in one hand she held an empty popcorn container with a drink container inside of that.

"Well, you shouldn't be driving then," she said. "There's a bed and breakfast down the block if you need a place to stay."

Everly Falls must be one of those places where everyone knew everyone. "I have a place, thanks." He took a step forward, expecting the woman to step out of the way, but she didn't move.

He supposed he could go down the opposite way.

"Oh, sorry," the woman said. "I didn't mean to hold you hostage or anything." She took a step back, then turned and moved along the row.

Austin followed at a bit of a distance. In her wake, he could smell whatever perfume she was wearing. Or was it her shampoo, or lotion? Whatever it was, it was sweet, and quite nice.

He kept his gaze up, not on her swaying hips or those heeled sandals of hers.

She walked quickly, and he was surprised at her speed. He wondered how long she had waited to wake him up because when he reached the lobby, the entire place was empty. Not a single employee was in sight.

The woman had already reached the exit doors, and she pushed through them without looking back. Austin decided there must be someone coming to lock up later, so he left the building too.

"Oh!" a woman exclaimed.

The same woman . . . Austin looked over and saw that she had fallen on the curb leading to the parking lot.

"Are you okay?" he asked as he strode over, although she was already sitting up and didn't appear injured.

"Oh no," she muttered and began to scramble on the ground. Her giant purse had spilled.

"I can help," Austin said, crouching to gather what looked like small squares of paper.

"Careful," she said. "Don't let them get bent."

"What are these?" Austin asked, holding one up so he could read the printed words in the outside lights of the movie theater. It was a movie ticket stub.

"My movie stubs," she said, then rose to her feet and chased after a couple that were blowing in the breeze. "My box must have popped open when I dropped my bag."

She returned, out of breath, her hair even more wild, her breathing hard.

Austin handed her what he'd gathered.

"Thanks," she said, tucking them into what looked like a plastic pencil box. "I'd hate to lose my collection."

Austin should probably head to his truck, but he'd never heard of a grown woman collecting movie stubs. "How long have you been collecting?"

Her gaze lifted to his, and he was pretty sure he'd never seen eyelashes that long. At least not natural ones. Rachel had been all about the fake eyelashes until she developed some sort of allergy to the glue.

"Since my first movie."

Austin's brows popped up. "You have all the stubs in there from every movie you've ever attended?"

"No," the woman said. "These are about two years' worth. I wouldn't carry around that many movie tickets."

Austin didn't know if he should laugh or continue staring at her. "You're kind of a movie buff, huh?"

She set her box inside her bag, then shouldered it and met his gaze. "I'm a secret movie buff," she said. "That's why I'm here on Wednesday nights. Place is mostly empty."

"Do you always sit in the middle seat, in the middle of the theater?" he asked.

She smiled.

Her smile was beautiful.

Which was something he probably shouldn't be noticing. Along with how he was rather enjoying her flowery scent. And . . . he took a step back because he suddenly realized how close he was to this stranger.

"I do." She tilted her head. "And you? I almost thought you were going to ask me to move."

He laughed. "I wouldn't, because that would be rude."

She was still smiling. "It is the best seat in the theater."

"Agreed."

She folded her arms, and the series of bracelets along her arms jangled. "Are you new in town? Passing through?"

"Neither," he said. "I'm here to renovate the theater."

Heather B. Moore is a *USA Today* bestselling author of more than ninety publications. Heather writes primarily historical and #herstory fiction about the humanity and heroism of the everyday person. Publishing in a breadth of genres, Heather dives into the hearts and souls of her characters, meshing her love of research with her love of storytelling.

Her historicals and thrillers are written under pen name H.B. Moore. She writes women's fiction, romance and inspirational non-fiction under Heather B. Moore, and . . . speculative fiction under Jane Redd. This can all be confusing, so her kids just call her Mom. Heather attended Cairo American College in Egypt and the Anglican School of Jerusalem in Israel. Despite failing her high school AP English exam, Heather persevered and earned a Bachelor of Science degree from Brigham Young University in something other than English.

For book updates, sign up for Heather's email list:
hbmoore.com/contact
Website: HBMoore.com
Facebook: Fans of Heather B. Moore
Blog: MyWritersLair.blogspot.com
Instagram: @authorhbmoore
Pinterest: HeatherBMoore
TikTok: https://www.tiktok.com/@heatherbmooreauthor
Twitter: @HeatherBMoore

www.ingramcontent.com/pod-product-compliance
Lightning Source LLC
LaVergne TN
LVHW021810060526
838201LV00058B/3314